Wrecked

A Taboo Romance

Kinsley Kincaid

EBOOK ISBN: 978-1-7389892-2-5

PRINT ISBN: 978-1-0688482-7-8

PRINT ISBN: 978-1-7389892-3-2

Editing and Proofreading: Book Witch Author Services

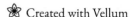 Created with Vellum

You are strong. You are worthy.
You are a fucking warrior.

Note From Author

Please be aware this book contains many **dark themes** and subjects that may be uncomfortable/unsuitable for some readers. This book contains **heavy themes** throughout. Please keep this in mind when entering Lily & Jaxson's story. Content warnings are listed on authors' social pages.

This book and its contents are entirely a work of fiction. Any resemblance or similarities to names, characters, organizations, places, events, incidents, or real people are entirely coincidental or used fictitiously.

If you find any genuine errors, please reach out to the author directly to correct it. Thank you.

ADDITIONAL NOTE

Should you or someone you know be struggling and
need support, please contact your local Mental Health
Helpline and/or Medical Professional.
Additional information and Resources can also be
found at
https://checkpointorg.com/global/

PLAYLIST

Spotify Playlist

Anxiety - Julia Michaels, Selena Gomez
Afraid - The Neighbourhood
Someone You Loved - Lewis Capaldi
Just Pretend - Bad Omens
Empty - Letdown.
Pain - Nessa Barrett
Lovely - Billie Eilish, Khalid
Wake Me up When September Ends - Green Day
We Can't Stop - Miley Cyrus
Milkshake - Kelis
Dog In Your Purse - Hannah Hill
Unholy - Miley Cyrus
Insanity - ILLENIUM, American Teeth

PILL BREAKER - Trippie Redd, Travis Barker,
Machine Gun Kelly, blackbear
papercuts (album edit) - Machine Gun Kelly
Watch The World Burn - Falling In Reverse
Fix You - Coldplay
Lonely - ILLENIUM, Chandler Leighton
Fire Meet Gasoline - Sia
Let It Go - Chandler Leighton, Lo Spirit
Nightlight - ILLENIUM, Annika Wells
sincerely - Nessa Barrett
Rise Up - Andra Day
My Mind & Me - Selena Gomez

CHAPTER 1

LILY

"Mom, Dad. I'm home." I yell, closing the front door of our trailer and dropping my school bag on the ground.

Living in the only trailer park in town isn't as bad as it sounds. Most people leave us alone. No one wants to be caught dead here unless they have no choice but to live here. Even then, some people that live here are embarrassed. I'm not. I kind of love it here. It's not a lot, but we get by. My dad does odd jobs for people and gets paid in cash. Mom watches the neighbor's kids during the day while I am at school.

Our trailer is your standard single-wide with a small living room off the kitchen. Down the narrow wood-paneled hallway are two smaller bedrooms, one is mine, the other is a spare room. Then, there's a third room; it's the master. We all share the one full bathroom. It's not glamorous, but it's home.

Strangely, I still don't hear anything as I wander inside.

I have bad anxiety. My parents both know that sudden changes in routine or unexpected events trigger my anxiety. It's always been bad, and it's something I have always dealt with, but it has only gotten worse as I have gotten older.

For neither of them to not be here or at least let me know they have gone out somewhere is out of character for them, and it automatically sends me into a panic.

Looking into the front room where the tv and couch are, there is nothing. Walking past the kitchen, down the narrow hall. I look into their room; it is unusually tidy and there is no one. The bed is made, the clutter that is ever-present on their bedside tables is missing. Even the nicknacks are gone from the old wooden dresser.

Something isn't right.

Turning out of their room, I go to mine. My black cat, Jinx, is sleeping on my unmade double bed. Everything is still in its place from this morning before I left for school. My drawings are still taped to the wall. My clothes are still in piles on the floor.

Feeling desperate, I check the bathroom. The

medicine cabinet is empty. Their pills, all their toiletries, my dad's razor, both toothbrushes are all gone. Everything is gone.

My brain immediately goes into overdrive.

It's racing a mile a minute trying to understand.

What is going on?

I grab my phone from my pants pocket, and there's no missed calls or notifications.

Yelling for them again, "Mom! Dad! Where are you?" As I walk out of the bathroom, back down the hall. I peek out the front door window.

Crap, my dad's car wasn't in the driveway when I walked up. Maybe they went out? Or maybe dad is still on a job?

I send a text to mom's phone. It comes back unable to deliver.

Heading back outside, I go to our neighbor's trailer, Janice. Mom watches her son sometimes.

I walk the short twenty feet to the home that is a near mirror image of ours, and knock on Janice's door.

Maybe she's heard from mom. I knock again.

Waiting a few more moments, I go to knock again when the door opens. Janice has her baby son, Lip, on her hip. "Hey, uh, Janice. Sorry to bother you. But my parents aren't home. I was wondering if maybe you have spoken to my mom today? I tried texting her, but it didn't go through."

"Yeah. I asked her to watch Lip today for a few hours so I could pick up some hours at the club, but she said she couldn't. Was busy. I saw her and your dad leave a few hours after that."

Nodding my head, trying to think. My mom never passes up baby-sitting hours. Every dollar counts.

"Oh, ok. Thank you Janice. They must have gone out. They didn't message me is all." I say, before walking back to my trailer.

Maybe something urgent came up. For them to not even message me or call. It has to be something urgent.

But all their things are gone. I checked every-where.... Wait. Their closet.

I walk through the front door and run to their room again, immediately going to the closet and opening it. Just like the rest of the house, it's empty. Their clothes are gone. Everything is gone. Only empty wire hangers remain. Turning around, I go to the dresser and open the drawers. Nothing.

My heart rate picks up even more. Racing so hard, it feels like it could explode out of my chest at any moment.

My breathing becomes uneven. Closing my eyes tight and grabbing my head with my hands. I don't understand. Did someone take them? Did they leave? Why didn't they tell me?

Maybe there's a note? There has to be a note.

I look on their bed and see nothing. Opening the bedside tables and the same thing. Empty.

Maybe they left it on the fridge?

Back down the hallway to the kitchen. I barely notice the old, thinning linoleum floor, passing by the cheap light wood and cream countertops as I urgently rush to the fridge. I look to the left where the fridge is and I see it. A magnet with an envelope that has my name on it, 'Lily' in mom's handwriting.

I feel myself start to shake even more and my stomach immediately drops.

I slowly make my way towards it, grabbing it off the fridge.

What have you two done?

CHAPTER 2

LILY

I've been sitting on this old brown couch for I don't even know how long. I've lost track of time and I'm not sure I even care anymore. Jinx sensed something was wrong; he always seems to know when I'm upset. He's curled up next to me now, sleeping while he tries to calm me. A lot of the time it works. Usually, just petting and cuddling with him relaxes me.

But this time, it's different.

I haven't opened the envelope. It is still sitting sealed on the worn coffee table in front of me. My black converse lie in a pile on the floor under the table; I kicked them off hours ago, or maybe it was minutes. I don't know. I can't help but sit here, staring at my name on the envelope, my legs crossed and I've pulled the hood of my oversized sweater over my head, as if I can hide from what is happening. Rocking back and forth on the couch to build up the courage and momentum to lean forward and pick it up again.

Maybe if I just opened the envelope, it would stop. My mind would shut off. The spiraling would end.

But I can't bring myself to do it yet. Opening it would make this real. Whatever this is.

Closing my eyes at the thought, I feel the tears that have been pooling in my eyes begin to slide down my cheeks. One tear tracks its way down to the corner of my mouth. I lick the sad, salty water away and it takes my mind off the situation if only for just a moment.

They haven't come back. Opening the envelope might tell me where they are. Or not.

They haven't called. They haven't texted. If I want to know anything, all I have to go off of is right here in front of me.

I tried calling them after I grabbed it off the fridge, hoping to hear from them what was going on. It went straight to the automated voice, telling me that she is 'sorry, but the number I am calling is no longer in service'. Thinking I may have dialed the wrong number, I tried again seven more times. She's sorry every time.

That's when my heart dropped into my stomach for the second time that afternoon. I bet that robot lady didn't know the effect she would have on people when she said those words. My breathing is uneven, and I can't seem to level it out. Usually, when my anxiety is triggered, I would inhale and exhale. Think happy thoughts. Rational thoughts. But there is nothing rational about any of this.

I thought we were happy. I was happy.

We struggled financially, sure. But we were happy. Right? Just mom, dad and me.

I'm questioning everything. Trying to think back. Were there signs that I missed? What could I have done better? Differently? I never got in trouble at school. I minded my business. I got picked on for being poor, but I never retaliated. If anything, I ignored those assholes that made fun of me because of where I lived and the cheap clothes I wore. I kept my head down. Did well in all my classes and put all my anger and emotion into my drawings.

I accepted all of it and never once asked for anything more than I knew they could give. Never once did I complain. I knew how important what little money we did have was. It paid the bills, bought groceries, and kept our trailer fees paid for. If we ever had anything extra, it went into the jar.

Mom and dad had a jar for 'rainy days'. Just in case dad didn't get enough odd jobs that month, they could use what was in there to help get by.

My mind won't stop racing with what if's and what could have's. Fuck it. Be brave Lil. Just open it.

My brain is screaming at me. But I'm a coward. I just want to run from what's inside of it. It didn't happen if I didn't see it. All of this will go away if I don't open it.

Finally, after taking a deep breath in, I open my eyes. Reaching my trembling hand out. I can't control it. It shakes and shakes as I reach for the envelope; it is so close but feels impossibly far away. Then, bringing it close to me. I smell her, the store brand jasmine and vanilla hand lotion my mom has always worn. It makes me smile at the thought of it.

Then I decide it's time.

Lily,

You have probably noticed by now we aren't home.

We left, Lil. We won't be back.

Raising you for the last 17 years has given us the greatest joy. We are so proud of you. We know you will do great things. Use your art to take you there.

It's our time to live now. Our job here is done.

The lot fees on the trailer are paid

for the next two months. It should get you to the summer and your birthday. From there, you'll need to get a job once school is over and keep paying them on your own.

I have canceled our phones. You won't be able to reach us. Please don't bother to try. We didn't take this decision lightly. This was necessary for us.

We need to do this for ourselves. To find ourselves as individuals again and not just parents.

We know you're probably panicking right now, Lil.

Just breathe, my girl. You are strong!

We love you always,
Mom & Dad.

CHAPTER 3

LILY

I t's 3am on a Tuesday morning. I should be sleeping because school starts in a few hours. Instead, I'm lying in the bathtub with warm water filled up to the edge. My feelings are floating away from me. I'm not the same person I was thirty days ago.

There was a party at Ethan's, a few trailers over. He has lived in the park for a few years now, but my parents told me to stay away from him, never go near his trailer. He's always hosting parties that I never attended–until recently. I can hear my dad's voice now, *'I tell you, that boy is up to no good.'*

Oh dad, if you only knew. Over the years, I would hear whispers that Ethan was maybe a drug dealer, or into that sort of lifestyle. You would see people going in and out of his trailer, no matter the time of day. But back then, I'd kept to myself. Never asking questions and kept my distance from anyone who ran in those sorts of circles. I always told myself the less trouble I caused for my parents, the less stress they would have. At least, that's how I thought of it. Turns out it was all bullshit. No matter what I did or didn't do, they would have left anyway. None of it even mattered. Not since they turned my life upside down and inside out. I don't care.

The first week my parents left, I still went to school and continued to keep to myself. It was just me and Jinx against the world.

Then, one night, I heard the pounding of music. Knowing exactly where it was coming from, and being curious with no one to stop me, I decided I needed to see for myself exactly what happened over there.

I crept through the bushes out back in the dark of the night until I reached Ethan's trailer. There were a few cars in the gravel driveway and a handful of people on the dimly lit deck talking and smoking. It didn't smell like normal cigarette smoke, though. Whenever the front door would open, I could hear the music more clearly and the faint voices of others from inside.

I was about to turn back to my place, not seeing anything interesting other than it being a party, when someone caught sight of me.

He was tall, with brown shaggy hair, wearing tight blue torn jeans, a black hoodie and black sneakers. He looked in my direction and yelled, "Who's back there?"

I didn't respond, hoping he would think it was just a tiny animal or something. It didn't work.

"I said, who is back there?" he yelled again, more firmly this time.

Squeezing my eyes shut, I internally cursed myself.

Busted.

"Uh, hi. It's Lily from a few trailers over."

Please, just let me go home. Please, just accept my response and leave me be.

"Lily, what are you doing back there? Come on out, you're not in trouble, sweetness," he said in a calm and friendly voice.

I debated just running off, but he knows where I live, so it would have been pointless. Taking a few steps forward from the bush, I showed myself.

"Ah, see sweetness, that wasn't too bad, was it? Now, tell me, what is a little girl like you doing sneaking around the park? It can get dangerous after dark."

"Um, I'm sorry. I just wanted to see. I always hear

music or people talking... I wanted to see for myself," telling him honestly, my curiosity got the best of me.

"See what for yourself?" He raises his eyebrow. I know he knows what I mean, but he is forcing me to say it out loud. Damn him.

"The parties. What all the talk was about around the parties. I just wanted to see. I won't tell anyone what I saw. Really, I didn't see anything, and I won't mention a word. I swear it." Getting the words out as quickly as possible.

He starts laughing. Is he laughing at me? I'm not sure. All I want to do is leave. "You're right Lily, you didn't see anything because there wasn't anything to see. Now, if you really want to see something, come back next weekend for a better look. Let your curiosity take over. You will hear the music when it's time, then you come back here and I will show you anything you want to see, ok sweetness?"

"Um, I really shouldn't. I can't. I'm actually going to go now, if that's ok, Ethan?" Please let me leave.

"Ok, you get home and stay home. No more sneaking out tonight, and lock your door. You hear me, Lily?" His tone is more authoritative now, it tells me he isn't fucking around.

"Yes. Of course." I quickly respond to Ethan while nodding my head, my eyes are completely wide. I don't want to know anymore, I won't question it. My heart is racing, and it feels like it might burst from my chest. I just need to get back home.

"Ok, sweetness. Go on," encouraging me to leave.

Without hesitation, I take off running.

After rushing back home that night, I did exactly as Ethan said, locked the doors and didn't sneak out again. After rushing into my room, I even locked that door, and then snuggled up with Jinx for the night.

The following weekend, I heard the music again, just like he said would happen. There was no chance I was going to go. That first night scared me. It almost triggered an anxiety attack after Ethan caught me.

But as the hours passed, while I sat at my desk sketching. I could hear the music beating loudly over the sound of Jinx on my bed, snoring. He lives the good life.

A familiar song comes on and I catch myself tapping my foot to the beat against the carpet.

Maybe it wouldn't hurt just to go and listen to some music? What's so wrong with that? Being under-age, it's not like I could do anything else. Or get into trouble.

Getting up, and grabbing my jean jacket, I throw it over my white crop tee and high-waisted jean shorts. I untuck my straight, long black hair from the collar and head out the door.

That was the first party I went to. Just a couple of

weeks after my parents so generously abandoned me. I'm only seventeen-fucking-years-old. What rational set of parents decide it's ok to leave their daughter alone? Fuck, I guess that's beside the point now.

I lost my virginity to one of his friends that night at the party, Luke. Turns out, they are best friends.

I was naïve back then, thinking because I'm underage that nothing could happen. Ethan's party is a place where the law doesn't exist. Anything you want, you can have. And I took it.

Luke is maybe around twenty. I don't remember and I never actually asked. Ethan immediately saw me walking up his drive from where he was standing on the deck. He took me under his arm, like a big brother. I felt safe. We walked around his trailer and he introduced me to everyone, some girls who seemed nice enough and some of his guy friends. He made it clear to his best friend, Luke, that he needed to watch out for me and to take care of me. And that he did.

I don't think I had ever had so much fun before. The music was still playing, so we danced. He stood behind me, holding onto my waist as we moved together to the beat. A few songs passed, and he asked if I was thirsty, looking back at him, I nodded. A cold drink was exactly what was needed, I was getting hot and sweaty.

All he had to do was snap his fingers and then two

bottles of beer were placed in his tattoo covered hands. He held one out to me, and not wanting to be rude, I took one. The first sip was disgusting. Luke laughed and swore it would only get better the more I had.

Hours passed. I didn't like beer, even after I finished the bottle, so he made me a vodka soda. Now that was delicious.

Luke made sure I only had two of those. He could tell this was my first time, or had assumed that from my reaction to the beer he gave me. I was surprised though, at how much of a gentleman he was being. I also was crushing on him—hard. He was hot. His hair was shaved down close to his skull, and he had tattoos all over. A tight black tee stretched over his chest and showed off his build physique, complete with black torn jeans and combat boots.

At one point, we made our way to the couch. He was talking to a few people around us, while I kept to myself, not knowing anyone. Luke had put his arm around my shoulders and I snuggled up right into him. He smelled so good it was intoxicating. It was a mixture of earthy and musk tones.

The music was still blasting, and people were having a great time. If this is what being drunk feels like, I never want it to stop. There's no feeling of anxiety, even around all these strangers. My mind and body felt more relaxed than it ever had before. I was having the time of my life. So, with this new and exciting feeling taking over, I decided I was going to kiss Luke.

Looking up at him, he turned his head, and looked back at me, so that's when I did it. I leaned in and kissed him. He immediately placed his other hand on my cheek and kissed me back, pulling me closer to him. He parted my lips with his tongue, and I let him in. Having never been kissed before it all could have gone terribly wrong, but instinct took over and I kissed him back. Our tongues touched, brushing against each other. It felt so fucking good. With each pass, it became more passionate, intense, and consuming.

He pulled back, keeping his lips just barely touching mine. "Are you sure you want this?" he whispered.

"Yes," telling him while looking straight into his eyes. I wanted to experience it all.

My response made him smile. I was so screwed. And he knew it.

Luke stood up and took my hand so I would get up to follow, and I did. He led us into a room down the hall, closed the door, and asked one more time. "Are you sure? Once this happens, we can't go back, Lil?"

He was being dead serious. I was shocked, not at all expecting him to ask and make sure this was still ok.

But, being absolutely sure, I grabbed the hem of

my white tee and pulled it off. It turns out that being drunk gave me the courage I would not normally have, and with that, again I said, "Yes."

He took it easy on me, knowing that it was my first time. I'd heard that first-time sex is never good, but this was way more awkward than I'd been expecting. Once we were finished, my buzz was wearing off, and I wasn't sure what to do next.

I was sick of feeling anything at all. I needed to get the monsters inside my head under control. The ones that caused me to overthink or worry and spiral. The loneliness I felt day after day in that trailer. I didn't want to feel again. Left alone in a trailer that no longer felt like home. Instead, I'm riddled with memories I wanted to forget. The what if scenarios that I played over and over again. My anxiety that constantly crept up on me. I hated it all. Luke told me he could help make it all go away.

So, I lost my drug virginity too.

Best night of my fucking life. I forgot everything terrible about my life.

Weed and Vodka. Turns out that I really enjoy them. I had a few more drinks after we cleaned up and got dressed. We went outside together where he lit a joint, and after a few hits, he held it out to me and I took it. The first hit was hard; my throat and lungs burnt and I couldn't stop coughing. After laughing at me, understanding that I was clearly new to this too, Luke explained little puffs to start until I got used to it. Taking his advice, that's what I did.

Best night of my fucking life.

I forgot everything terrible about my life.

I just got home thirty minutes ago. Lying back in the warm water of the tub, I can tell I'm fucked up in more ways than I can count right now. I tried Oxy tonight for the first time. After Luke and I fucked again, he offered me one. We do that a lot now, fuck, and it's gotten so much better since the first time.

I have never mixed drugs before, but I suppose there is a first time for everything. When I asked him what it was like, Luke said, 'if you want to be numb, this is what will do it.'

So, I took it, the whole thing. Not giving a fuck about the consequences. I'm done feeling.

Within minutes, that is exactly how I felt. It was like my brain went tingly and dazed first, then the rest of my body followed. I'm sure if someone slapped my face, I wouldn't have felt it. Or even been phased by it.

Turns out, Ethan is a dealer. A massive one. It's none of my business, and the less I know, the better. But, I found that out after a hook up with Luke. I asked him and he simply said, 'what do you think?' taking the hint I didn't ask anymore questions about it.

One perk of fucking the drug dealer's best friend is that I don't have to pay for these trips. Or at least not yet, not with anything other than sex. I'm sure he has other girls he does this with, but I don't care. We are all just using each other to get what we need, when we need it. This is the side of the world I'd never been exposed to before. But now I genuinely feel like this is the part of the world I belong to. It was always supposed to be like this. It wasn't a life before. All I did was run from myself.

Still feeling the effects of everything in my body. My mind is still dazed, the euphoric rush of the Oxy has settled in and I am numb. Taking a deep breath in, air begins to fill my lungs.

I probably shouldn't be taking a bath when I'm this high. But here we are.

My parents shouldn't have left me. But again, here we are. Making lemons into lemonade, they say.

That's exactly what I'm doing—making the best of a bad situation—and I feel more alive than ever before. This is who I am now. This is the true Lily. This is who I was meant to be.

With Green Day's 'Wake Me When September Ends' playing in the background, I submerge myself under the water. Opening my eyes, I look up through the water and focus on one spot on the ceiling. I wonder how long I can hold my breath before I pass out? Would anyone even notice I was gone? Would they come looking for me? Or would my body shrivel up in the water for days and weeks before anyone noticed I was gone?

When they finally found me, would they have a funeral or a party? What would they do with my body? I think about these things more now than I ever had. It doesn't scare me. I am curious. What happens to your soul after you die? Is it released from the struggles of depression and anxiety? It is finally free and happy once it reaches the so-called after life? One day, I will find all my answers.

My lungs start to contract; I'm running out of air.

Do I sit up, or do I stay here like this and find my answers now?

My chest tightens more, and I let my lungs struggle for another few seconds before deciding to emerge from the water.

Sitting up, my eyes still on that spot above me, I let the water run down my face as I rapidly take in desperately needed breaths. My hair is slicked back from the water and my mascara is no doubt running down my face. Bracing myself on the tub's edge, I lean forward, still trying to catch my breath. It feels like I'm hyperventilating when I play this game.

It's my own version of Russian roulette. Will she stay under or will she get up? Each time I play it, I don't know what I will do until the very last second. The rush is what has me hooked. This is how I live now.

This is something else I have fallen in love with.

CHAPTER 4

LILY

I'm laying in my double bed with my eyes still closed, while patting around to find my phone, not bothering to open my eyes yet. I would sleep the entire day away if I could, but as much as I love that idea, there is someone relentlessly knocking on my front door.

Jesus fuck, go away.

Finally, I locate my phone and see it's almost noon. Shit, I should wake up. Once I've thrown back the thin bed sheet that I was comfortably sleeping under, I roll out of bed, with Jinx looking at me like I'm the rude one disturbing our sleep. The weather is already getting hot for mid-spring in Michigan and I'm only in my white tank top and black panties. Without air conditioning or fans, the only way to keep cool in the trailer is to wear barely anything. It's too damn warm to care and if you are going to bother me at home right now, this is what you get.

Making my way down the short hallway, I unlock the front door, and open it. It takes a moment for my eyes to adjust to the bright sun shining on me, and I see it's my older cousin, Jaxson. Shit, he has to be twenty-one now. Jaxson is wearing baggy tan work pants, a white tee and a pair of black steel toe work boots. The guy is built and covered in tattoos. He has black wavy hair which is short on the sides and longer on top and hangs over his forehead. But it's his eyes that always catch my attention, one green and the other one hazel. They are the most unique and beautiful eyes I've ever seen. You can get lost looking into them.

I don't want him catching me admiring him, so I let out a yawn, and don't bother to cover my mouth. He hasn't said anything yet; he is just staring at me with his expression slowly changing as he takes me in. So, I decide we should get this family reunion with my cousin over and done with. "Jax, what are you doing here?"

He looks mortified.

"Lil, put some fucking clothes on. And don't answer the door like this again," he snaps at me, while waving his tattooed hands around.

I'm in no mood for this today.

"Shit, fine whatever. But what are you doing here?"

It's a legitimate question. He never comes over, so I have no idea what he really wants. Hoping the sooner I can get that information out of him, the sooner he is on his way out of here.

"I need to borrow a few tools for a last-minute job. Is your dad around?" He asks while still looking unimpressed. Is he always this unpleasant, or is it just me that brings this side out of him?

"Does it look like he's around, Jax?" I throw back at him. "His car is not in the driveway and I am very obviously only just waking up. Of course, he isn't here."

"What's gotten into you? Shit, Lil. Wait, why aren't you at school?" He is slowly starting to put it together.

"No Jaxson, my dad isn't home. My mom also isn't home. Do you see their car in the driveway? You can check the back shed for the tools you're looking for, but if what you need isn't there, I can't help you." I shrug him off and hope this gets him out of here as fast as possible.

He just looks at me. His face is blank. I can't be sure what he's thinking, so I start closing the door. This conversation is done, I have nothing else to say.

The door is almost closed when his hand reaches out and stops it. Wrapping his tattooed knuckles around the door.

"I don't think so, Lil. What the fuck is going on here? You're answering the door practically naked. You aren't in school, and frankly, you look like shit." He says. It's so abrupt, I can't tell if it's sarcasm or something else.

"Fuck you, Jax. As much as I want to say, I appreciate your observations, I don't. Now, get what you need and leave, please." I hope this works and he just goes away.

"I don't think so. Explain. Where are your parents and what the fuck is going on? The last time I saw you, you were not this," he sneers as he looks me up and down.

"Oh, and exactly what does that mean?"

My arms are now crossed over my chest. I don't handle confrontation well. Almost immediately I get defensive. It also triggers my anxiety, but whatever I took last night must still be in my system because I only feel slightly annoyed by this situation. My usual reactions aren't coming out, thank fuck.

"The last time I saw you, your eyes didn't look bloodshot, with dark circles around them and caved in. You weren't acting like a miserable bitch and presumably skipping school." With each statement, his tone gets more harsh.

"Flattering. Always a charmer, Jaxson Reed," I spit

back at him. I've stopped caring about this conversation. It is time to wrap it up. But apparently what I've said has really pissed him off. Jax is now pushing his way inside by holding the door open with one hand and using his other to block me from pushing him back out. He slides past me and makes his way to the kitchen.

The house is a mess. I haven't kept up with the cleaning; I didn't care enough to. There are dishes piled in the sink, and weed scattered all over the top of the coffee table, along with a few bottles and take out bins. Sometimes Luke comes over here and we have our own parties. Shit, I don't need Jax knowing any of this. He is already far too invested in this situation as it is, and he knows absolutely nothing about it.

As if on cue, Luke walks in. *Mother fucker, could my day get any worse?* I close my eyes and take a deep breath in as I feel my heart rate start to pick up.

"Babe, whose truck is in your driveway? Are your parents back?" Luke casually asks, completely oblivious to Jaxson's presence. This entire situation is fucked. I exhale my breath slowly before reopening my eyes to try to stop my anxiety that's building. I hate this feeling. The stress and build up to what is about to happen is sometimes worse than the actual anxiety attack that comes after. I look at Jax and respond to

Luke "No, it's my cousin's truck. He came by to borrow tools from my dad, he was just leaving."

"Wait, back up a minute. What did he mean, are your parents back?" Jax asks while looking around.

"Nothing, let it go." I sigh, hoping he accepts my answer.

"No. Tell me what the fuck this half wit meant. Now, Lily!" he demands.

"Whoa bro, don't talk to her like that." Luke casually jumps in. I wish he would just shut up and leave. The guy isn't that bright, and by the tone of his voice, he is also very high.

"Stay out of this. I'll talk to her any way I like. Now fuck off and leave." Jaxson spits back at Luke, looking deadly, like he could snap at any moment.

"No, Luke can stay. Whatever you need to say can be said in front of him too." I know Luke should go, but also knowing he is pissing my cousin off makes me want him to stick around a little longer. Could be worth the anxiety attack that is about to hit.

"Is this ass fuck why you are like this now, Lil?" he questions, while pointing to Luke.

Having enough of his accusations, "*I'm* why I'm like this, Jax. I've grown up since the last time you saw me. This is me now, so take it or leave it. I don't really care."

"Where are your parents? What did he mean? Are they back?" My cousin questions again.

Luke takes that moment to open his mouth again, "They left her. Her family fucking left her and no one came to save her but me. No one's been looking out for her but me. So get what you need, and fuck off. We are fine here." My eyes are wide. Luke has no idea what he did now.

Jax goes deadly still. No expression on his face, but his chest is moving rapidly, like he is going to explode.

My dad told me a bit about Jax and how he can be a hot-head. That he's been known to lash out, and beat the shit out of people when provoked. As soon as the thought leaves my head, Jax reaches his arm out and wraps his strong hand around Luke's neck. His tattooed forearm strained while pushing him against the wall. Fuck.

Rushing up behind Jax, I put my hands gently on his arm in an effort to calm the situation. "Jax, let him go. Let him go and he will leave. We can talk, then you can leave. How does that sound?" I plead, then quickly look at Luke so he knows to go along with whatever I'm saying. I'm trying to avoid a complete blood bath happening in my trailer. Not to mention, a full-blown attack that I am trying to convince myself to not have right now. I haven't had anything since last night, and now I'm starting to feel everything. Shit.

"Yeah, man, I meant no disrespect. Just let me go and I'll take off." Luke pleads as my cousin continues to choke him. It takes a few moments before Jax decides to let go of him.

He slowly unwraps his fingers from Luke's neck and takes a couple of steps backward. Jax is still staring at Luke like he could tear him apart in a blink of an eye. His nostrils are flaring when he says in a harsh whisper that leaves no room for argument. "Get. The. Fuck. Out. Now!"

I look at Luke, and mouth, *"hurry."* He needs to get out of here before my cousin really hurts him, or worse. Luke doesn't hesitate, and he takes off out the front door.

Slowly turning back to face me, Jaxson looks pissed, his face is red, "Explain Lil. What in the fuck have I walked into?"

What a fucking disaster. Walking over to the couch, I sit down with my hands trembling in my lap. Not wanting him to see how this is affecting me, I slide to the edge of the seat cushion, grab some of the loose weed from the coffee table and put it into a spare paper I had laying out. He's mortified and pissed, and I don't even have to bother looking up at him to know this. I don't care how he feels right now. Fuck, I continue to even my breathing out with the same deep breaths I've been doing since this has started, but it's not working. I can't roll this joint fast enough. It's not pretty once finished, but it will have to do. Grabbing the lighter in front of me before sitting back on the couch, I bring the joint to my lips. Once lit, I toss the lighter back on the coffee table.

I take a massive hit before initiating into conversation again. Blowing out a cloud of smoke, I start, "Mom and dad left about a month ago. Don't ask. I don't know where they went. I don't even want to talk about it. But since you won't leave, they were gone before I got home from school one day. All I do know is, they paid the trailer fees for a couple months, then it's up to me." I finish explaining as I take another hit.

Fuck, I'm feeling so much better already.

Looking up to where Jax is still standing. He hasn't said anything yet. He is just looking at me expectantly. I'm not sure what else he is waiting for, so I take another hit.

"Are you serious right now?" He shouts at me.

"Very. They aren't here." Not sure what else he needs to hear to understand. This isn't something anyone would joke about.

"Fuck's sake, Lil. I come here to see if your dad has a few tools I could borrow for this job—a job I am now late for—and find you like this. Why didn't you call anyone when this happened? I don't fucking understand." Why is he so concerned about me now? We aren't even close.

Taking one more hit of my joint before putting it out in the empty beer bottle in front of me, I look back up at Jax, "You should really get going if you're late. The sheds unlocked. Take whatever you need."

"You are such a bitch, do you know that? I am just trying to understand what the fuck is going on here. I'm going to leave, not because your little fucking act worked. But because I need to get back to work. I'm coming back later. We are going to talk about this. Be here. Or I'll fucking find you." He threatens, while pointing his finger at me. Fucking psychopath.

"Yeah. Ok cousin, you got it. Have a *great* day," I smile as the beautiful sound of sarcasm leaves my mouth.

Jaxson is doing everything in his power not to explode right now, it's hilarious. His face is getting red and his eyes are wide, nostrils flaring. His tattooed hands are clenched into tight fists and his knuckles are turning white. He has gorgeous ink; one hand has a rose on it and the other a skull, all in black and gray. But seeing them clenched like this tells me I have hit a nerve.

He finally decides to leave, and I begin to think that I have gotten the last word, but I'm wrong because he yells, "Put some fucking clothes on!" Then slams the front door closed behind him.

Fuck that, I'm just fine like this. Plus, I'm sure he isn't some saint either. Such a fucking hypocrite.

I wait until I hear Jaxson's vehicle start and drive away off the gravel driveway before I send a message to Luke letting him know it's safe to come back. If anyone can help take my mind off the day that has barely just begun, it's him. I toss my phone next to me and Luke walks in. He must not have gone far.

"Babe. That fucker is crazy. You know that?" His face is very serious, which makes me laugh. He is never serious. I think he is really scared of my cousin. The more I look at Luke, the harder I laugh. Tears are even running down my face from laughing so hard. His face doesn't change, he just takes it. Shit, I am so high. I can't stop laughing now.

"You're fucked up, aren't you? I'm being serious and you're laughing at me like a fucking hyena, Lil. You should know, I'm very serious. He's fucking insane. You should have seen the look in his creepy fucking eyes when he had me pinned against the wall. Fucking deranged. So, can you just please stop laughing now, babe?"

"I know. I know. I swear. It's just this entire situation. From my parents. To you. To me. And now my cousin. I can't cry over it. That gets me nowhere and solves nothing. This is my fucking life now, Luke. I swear you can't write this shit. So all I can do is laugh at the absurdity of it." Saying in between my giggle fit.

A smile starts to form on Luke's face. "You're not wrong, babe. Your life is completely fucked up. But don't worry, I got you. I'll help take care of you now." It's almost like he is sincere in his offering, so I go with it. Even though I know exactly what this is. We have sex, we do drugs, we pass time together. That is the only way we take care of each other in this fucking strange friendship.

"Hmm, I do like the sounds of that. But how about I take care of you right now? You have had such a stressful day." Arching my eyebrow at him and smirking.

Licking his lips, he walks over and stands next to where I am sitting. Slowly, he starts to undo his tight black jeans and pulls them down until they bunch at his feet. He doesn't wear underwear, and his cock is already hard. Then he takes a seat next to me, leaning all the way back on the couch. I get up from where I am and kneel in front of him. He spreads his legs wide for me and I crawl between them. Fuck, my mouth is watering already. I love giving head. The power you have when a man's dick is down your throat is indescribable. He is completely at my mercy. I own his orgasm.

Slowly licking my lips, then biting the bottom one with my teeth while making eye contact with him, I grab ahold of his thick cock and brush my thumb over the precum already leaking from his tip. I let go of him and bring my thumb up to my mouth and suck on it, his eyes are already hooded just watching me. "Hmm, you like that baby. You want me to suck your big cock, don't you, Lukey?" I like making him beg when I'm on my knees before him.

"Fuck ya babe. You suck him so well. He needs you," he encourages.

"Well, if he needs me, how can I say no, then?" With a final smile and a wink, I grab a hold of his hard length and begin to lick it from base to tip. I move slowly, causing him to shiver. Then, I bring my lips over his head, playing with the slit with my tongue. Causing him to grab my hair and force his cock further in my mouth and finally hitting the back of my throat. He starts to use me, thrusting his hips while his cock fucks my mouth. He is rough with each thrust.

Panting, he lets out, "Babe, stay still. Just like this. Let me have this. Let me use you."

Complying, I further relax my throat so he can get deeper. He does deserve this, since he was almost murdered by my cousin.

I can feel saliva starting to drip down my chin as he continues to thrust himself against the back of my throat. His pace is hard and fast, and I know he won't last much longer. I start to gag, causing him to moan, "Fuck. You're so beautiful like this. Gagging on my cock like a fucking mess. And it's all for me." Praising me as I continue to take his hard thrusts in my mouth.

"Babe, I'm about to cum. Sit back," he rasps as he lets go of my hair. Leaning back on my knees, I look up at him. I can still feel the drool dripping down my chin as I watch him now, working his cock with his hand, aiming it at me as he does. After a few pumps, his cum starts to shoot out on my face. Closing my eyes, I open my mouth so I can catch every drop I can. He is decorating me with his cum. A bit gets in my mouth and I lick my lips to get more of his salty release and swallow it. Most of it is on my forehead, I can feel it dripping down my face, covering my eyes and cheeks. Once the last bit of warm cum hits my face, I open my eyes, some noticeably in my eyelashes. Luke is looking back down at me with hooded eyes and biting his lip. "Don't clean it off. I want you to rub it in. I want you to feel me on you the rest of the day." I don't say anything, I don't need to, just smile and I do as I am told. Rubbing his cum all over my face with my hands. Rubbing it down to my neck, making sure none is wasted. I feel so much better now. My anxiety has long since left my body. The mixture of the weed and his release has helped take my mind off everything. I guess I needed this, too.

Sitting up from being on the floor, I move to the couch and lay my head opposite of where he is sitting, then curl up and turn on the tv. He grabs my feet, bringing them over his lap, and starts rubbing them. It always surprises me when he does nice gestures like this for me. I just don't expect it from him. It feels nice. I'd never admit this out loud, but I've missed being cared for.

Chapter 5

Jax

What in the fuck was that?

When I got up this morning, I figured I would stop by uncle's and borrow some tools. I definitely didn't think, *'Oh, I'll just drop by my uncles, see my hot, half-naked cousin answer the door, and maybe for shits and giggles almost beat the shit out of some asshole kid she is clearly fucking.'*

This morning. That is not the Lily I know. And Jake? Luke? Or whatever his fucking name is? The kid looks like a complete fucking tool. Who the fuck is she hanging around? Her parents would *never* allow any of this shit. I need to find out where the fuck her parents are. I could tell her anxiety was kicking up when I pressured her to talk about it.

My dad's brother has always run a tight ship, no sketchy fucks around his daughter. She has crazy anxiety and is super fucking awkward around people. But the version I saw of her, just now, showed no signs of any of that. She was half fucking naked opening the door. That didn't scream socially awkward to me. But, fuck, if she hasn't grown up since the last time I saw her. I didn't even check for the tools I'd come for and needed before leaving. I just needed to get out the fuck out of there, unable to be around her for another second. I swear I could feel my blood pressure rising and if I stayed any longer, I would have lost my fucking head. It's not even about the tools anymore. I'm just glad I stopped by. There's something not right going on over there. And I'm going to get to the bottom of it whether she likes it or not.

I wonder if my dad has heard anything about what the fuck is going. He and my uncle were never close, but he has to know something. My old pickup doesn't have the fancy tech all the new rides do, so I can't just ask my bluetooth to call him. I'll have to wait until I get the job site and hope he can give me some fucking answers.

It's almost 8pm. We normally do twelve-hour days once the temperature and daylight permits. Once winter hits, business slows right down.

I called my dad, and he had no idea what I was talking about when I asked him where his brother was. I explained to him only what he needed to know from what happened this morning. That Lily seemed to be alone in the trailer. He did say he would call around to see what he could find out for me.

Hours felt like years, waiting for my fucking phone to vibrate in my pocket. I'm sure I checked it every twenty minutes to make sure I didn't miss a call. Finally, I heard back from him only an hour ago. He tried calling my uncle, a number no longer in service. He also called a few guys he knows my uncle does odd jobs for, and they haven't seen him in almost a month, they figured. I told dad not to worry; he has a heart condition, and doesn't need extra stress in his life. I let him know that I would go back over to their place tonight and see what I can get out of Lily. Dad figures she has to be there alone, but found it strange that her dad and mom would just disappear without the other.

This is a complete fucking shit show. What kind of people just leave their kid like this? Just drop off the face of the earth, and for what? What could be more important to them than their fucking child? I didn't know my aunt and uncle were like this.

Thinking about it all again pisses me off. I hit my steering wheel out of frustration as I pull up to my place. I own a small two-bedroom house in town. After hanging up on my dad and taking some anger out on the site we are working on, I decided she is either coming home with me or I'm going to stay over there. I know she will put up a fight. I'd almost prefer it if she does. It's no issue for me, to have to force her into accepting that this is how it's going to be now.

Getting out of the truck, I slam the door, then walk up to my front door. Once I unlock it and head inside, I am a man on a mission, not even bothering to take my boots off as I walk through the kitchen and head straight to my bedroom closet. Grabbing my duffle bag from the top shelf , I start loading it with clothes from my closet and dresser drawers. Going to my bathroom next, I start loading up all the toiletries I'll need. My gut says it will be a bitch to get her to come here, so I may as well prepare to be a temporary resident at the trailer. Taking one more walk through, I make sure I have everything I may need, but still knowing I could always swing by tomorrow if anything is missed. Once the duffle bag is zipped up, I head back out, leaving the kitchen light on so people think maybe someone's home while I'm gone. It's not a rough area, but kids are shit wherever you live.

I lock up the house, throw my bag in the box of the

truck, and get in. Then, grabbing my pack of smokes from the dash, I stick one in my mouth and light it. This girl better be home and that tool better not be there when I arrive. I am not in the mood to deal with any of their bullshit.

Chapter 6

Lily

Sex is best on Ecstasy.

That's what Luke told me. So I said, what are we waiting for?

About forty-five minutes ago, he pulled a baggy out of his pocket, and it had the cutest little blue pills inside. Grabbing two out, he handed me one and without hesitating I put it in my mouth, swallowing it down with some water that I had grabbed earlier. He did warn me to stay hydrated when on this. Of course, I listened. He knows more than me about this stuff.

He took a pill right after me, and I'm not sure if his has kicked in yet, but mine has. Compared to the other drugs we've done–weed, Oxy and Xanax–I've noticed this is a gradual climb. It's not hitting me all at once, but as the minutes went by, I started to feel it more and more. It's like bursts of passion and energy entering my body, and I need to use it. I need to use it on Luke. Fuck, that man is beautiful. We are on the couch in the living room of my trailer. I reach my hand up, my head is laying on his lap. He looks down at me, and I start to caress his cheek. It's the most beautiful face I have even seen. His skin is incredibly soft. I can't stop touching him. I need more. Sitting and looking him in the eyes, I use both my hands to hold his face.

"Babe, I love when you touch me like this. Touch me more. Touch me everywhere." Luke pleads. I love when he begs for me.

"Hmm, Luke. You are so beautiful. I never want to stop touching you," and with that, I lean in and kiss him. We have music playing, but it's all background noise now. I feel like I'm finally living in the moment. This, right now, is the only thing that is going on in the world and I get to be in it. How fucking lucky am I? Here. Right now. It's only us.

With each inhale I take, the deeper I kiss him. He is supplying my oxygen. We are one person. Our tongues brush against each other, my covered breasts rubbing against his chest. I can't get close enough. His hands start to move from where they are at my hips to under my shirt. I lean back from our kiss and put my arms in the air; he knows what I am asking of him and pulls my shirt over my head with my bralette following and throws it to the ground. This feels so much better, free of any barrier between us. I take his shirt off next, exposing his beautiful chest and his abs that I have to lick at some point tonight. I crave the feeling of my tongue brushing against the ridges of his muscles.

I'm not sure how long I spend admiring his body, but he grabs my face and tilts my head up and starts kissing me again and I moan into his mouth. This is the most explosive experience. With each kiss, I crave another.

I need him to be more naked. I need to feel all of his skin against mine. Reaching down without breaking our kiss, I undo his jean button and slide down the zipper. I grab the sides and start to pull them down until he reaches down to take over. I watch as he lifts his hips and pulls his jeans down, and his hard cock is instantly exposed. My mouth is watering. I need him in my mouth. Standing up, I remove my panties. I'm still not dressed from this morning, wearing what I had on when I woke up and Jax was here. Kneeling in front of him, I lean in and slowly lick his abs, moving from his pelvis to just below his chest while bracing myself on his thighs. It's better than I even imagined. The feeling of his soft skin against my tongue and the ridges of his muscles are addictive. I use the tip of my tongue and slowly work my way down before I move my tongue to the tip of his cock. Precum is already leaking out. I swipe it over his head just once, as a tease. I get a taste of his salty release and immediately go back in for more. Grabbing his base with my tiny hands, I wrap my lips around his cock and slowly take him deeper. I couldn't move faster if I tried.

Savoring every fucking inch of him. This has to be an effect of Ecstasy. The feeling and the touching. The need to absorb and savor each movement we make. I cannot get enough of this. The sensation of his soft skin against my tongue, my teeth lightly brushing against his shaft causes me to moan. I need more, so much more. Letting go of his hard shaft, I start to rub his inner thighs and move slowly towards his balls, gripping them in my hand and rubbing them slowly. Hollowing out my cheeks, I take him as deep as I can; his cock hitting the back of my throat. This connection, right now, at this moment, is electric.

"Fuck babe, you feel so fucking good taking my cock like this," Luke moans.

He's right: this is the most amazing feeling. I want to please him, and I crave his praise. To feel and taste every inch of him. I move my hands from his balls back to his shaft and start to work his hard cock as my mouth continues to suck him back. He tastes so fucking good.

He grabs ahold of my hair to take him deeper and starts fucking my mouth. His hips pushing his cock against my throat as I start to gag. My eyes water, but I will not give up.

"Take it Lil, take it all," he demands with his husky voice. I will take it, I will not stop until I feel his cum at the back of my throat.

"I'm going to cum, and you're going to take it all. Fuck, you feel amazing, babe." I feel the rumble of his voice vibrate through me and that's when I feel his dick jerk and his orgasm hits. His cum is coating the back of my throat and I take every single drop. I stay like this, not resting until I feel the last of his orgasm dripping down my throat. He lets go of my hair and I look up at him and slowly move my mouth off his shaft. His eyes are full of lust when he looks down at me.

Sitting back on my heels, I lick my lips to ensure I got it all. But I need more, and so does he. He leans forward, grabs me by the underarms and lifts me onto his lap. Our lips crash together. My hands go to the back of his head to pull him closer to me as he holds my hips in place and starts grinding against my wet pussy. It's not enough though. I need to feel him inside of me, consuming every inch of my mind and body. Still kissing, I lean up and take his hard cock in my hand, lining it up with my entrance and slide down him as slowly as possible. The need to feel every single inch as it goes inside of me is overwhelming. You cannot get any closer than the two of us right now. Our passion is raw, and it's real.

I start moving my hips slowly at first when I feel a tingle of electricity inside of me. This is euphoric. I never want his hard cock to leave me, I grip it tighter with my pussy in order to feel him working me even more. I am never letting go. He is so deep inside of me; I have never felt this full before. Still not breaking our kiss, I moan into his mouth as he continues to work me. We never stop touching, and I can feel sweat drip from his forehead to my cheek. I lean back and lick his face; I love the salty taste on my tongue. He grabs my breasts and squeezes them. They aren't very big, each able to fit into his masculine hands. This causes me to arch my back while holding onto his shoulders, and I continue moving up and down on him.

"Fuck Luke, this feels so good. Squeeze them harder and don't stop until I say," I plead in barely a whisper. I'm panting so hard and know that I am just as sweaty as he is, but I don't care.

My orgasm begins to build. Holding onto his shoulders as tight as I can, I move even faster chasing it.

Throwing my head back as it hits, "Fuck. Do. Not. Stop. Never stop, keep going." I demand with each thrust. Finally, he lets go of my breasts, holds me down by my hips, and starts thrusting harder inside me. This feels incredible.

Opening my mouth, I let out a loud moan with my head still tilted back as I start cuming all over his cock. My pussy is coating it with my release, and that's when I feel him swell inside of me. We both work each other through our orgasms. His hot release mixing with mine. My back tingles with pleasure. I move my hands to his chest and start rubbing his wet, sweaty skin. This is amazing. Leaning forward, I start to kiss his neck, getting more of the delicious salty flavor that I love hitting my taste buds. That's when I think I hear another a voice yelling, "What the fuck is this?"

Convinced it's not real, and it's the Ecstasy playing tricks, we keep going. I open my eyes and look to the side, not seeing anyone. I'm finding it hard to focus with all the pleasure coursing through my body. It must have just been in my head, then suddenly a fist comes into my view and it connects with Luke's face. His eyes are still closed as he was riding out his own orgasm, and he doesn't have a chance to avoid it before it connects.

I turn my head to the other side of me, where the fist came from, and see my cousin standing next to me. What the fuck is Jax doing here?

CHAPTER 7

JAX

Parking my truck in front of the single-wide trailer, I get out and grab my bag from the back. I hear music coming from inside as I start to walk up to the door. Great, she's having a fucking party. It must be with other park kids since no other vehicles are around. Going up the wooden steps, I knock on the door a couple of times, waiting for someone to answer. No one answers. Fuck, this is ridiculous. Blowing a deep breath and preparing myself for what I am walking into, I grab the door handle and open it. There's no one there to see when I walk in at first, but the kitchen light is on. I drop my bag and close the door behind me, moving further into the trailer. Now, looking down the hallway, expecting her to come out of her room, when I yell, "Lily!"

Then, from behind me, I hear a loud moan.

Turning around, that's when I see it. Lily is naked. She is naked with her petite frame riding that fucking loser's dick. Her head is thrown back with her long black hair hanging down her back. Her body glistening with sweat. She has tiny breasts that are perky and her nipples are hard. She's beautiful.

And I am livid.

"What the fuck is this?"

They either didn't hear me or are ignoring me because they keep fucking. Walking forward, I clench my fist and, without a second thought, punch the son of a bitch in the face. You can hear the crack of the connection as soon as it meets his jaw. Lily turns her head and starts screaming, but I ignore her. I need this mother fucker out of this trailer and his tiny dick out of my cousin.

I don't see Lily anymore; everything turns black around me. It's tunnel vision now. All I see is this fuck face. He's holding his face with blood trickling through his fingers; it must be coming from his nose. If not, I will just have to punch him again. I want to beat his face in until he is no longer recognizable.

"Get up! Get your shit and get the fuck out of here!" I shout at him.

I swear to fuck. If he doesn't get out of here in the next 10 seconds, I will kill this kid. I'll call the police and put on my own handcuffs, but it will be fucking worth it.

But he's smart. He doesn't miss a beat. I finally notice Lily is no longer on him. She is now beside him, covering herself with her knees brought up to her chest. Oh, cousin, no need to hide from me. Ass-wipe is grabbing his shirt and pants with one hand, slips his shoes on, and runs naked through the door. I swear his dick is hidden inside him; you don't even see it when he takes off out of here like a pussy.

I turn my body and face Lily; she looks terrified. Her eyes are wide, her body shaking with cum dripping out of her. Fucking class act, cousin.

"Go clean yourself up, put some clothes on and get your ass back out here. We have shit to discuss. Got it?"

Faintly nodding her head, she gets up and scurries down the hall. I hear a door shut and the shower turn on.

She needs to fucking cleanse herself of that coward.

Needing to get my thoughts together, I take a look around. This place is a mess. Still no sign of Lily's parents anywhere. Jesus, fuck.

While I wait for Lily, I take a seat on the couch, not the cushion they were just fucking on, and see there's weed out on the coffee table and now a baggie of pills. What in the fuck. Picking up the baggie, I see they are blue pills with a crazy stamp in the middle of them.

I'm not a moron. These are Ecstasy pills. So what, now she does drugs? Taking pills? I bet that fucker is supplying her, too. No way Lily would know where to find this stuff on her own.

I throw the bag back on the table, and the pills clank against the top as they land. This entire situation is more fucked than I thought. She need to hurry the fuck up because the longer I sit here with this shit music playing and the image of her with him like that, the more pissed off I get.

Cracking my knuckles, I grab my smokes from my pocket and put one in my mouth. Finding a lighter on the coffee table to light it. Inhaling deeply, I feel the sweet taste of nicotine hit my lungs. This is exactly what I needed. Exhaling it out. I take another drag when I hear the bathroom door open. Choosing to ignore her, I don't look toward the sound. She will walk in here, embarrassed and hopefully still terrified as she should be.

"Um, Jax. What are you doing here?" her voice trembles. I bet she's sobered up quickly. After all, I did punch her boy toy while they were fucking. That would sober anyone up

Deciding not to respond, I suck back my cigarette and blow out a ring of smoke into the air. Hopefully this makes her sweat more.

"Jax. Answer me. What are you doing here?" She's getting a little braver with her tone.

"Are you on birth control? Do you need the morning-after pill? What are we dealing with here, Lil?"

I don't think she quite expected me to ask those questions, but this is my priority right now.

"No, I'm not on anything. I'll go to the store in the morning for the morning-after pill. Luke will take me. It's fine."

It's fine? Is she serious right now? None of this is fucking fine.

Finally looking up, I take her in from her black painted toes up her thin legs past her black cotton panties, white cropped shirt and long black hair. She is picking at her nails while I continue to look at her. Lily's face, it's too thin, her eyes look caved in with black bags around them. She's too thin. I need to get some food into this girl. If I were a stranger looking at her now, you would think she hadn't eaten in days. I didn't notice this when she was riding that moron's dick. The lighting was dim in the living room, but now that she is standing in the kitchen, I see everything. But I still think she's beautiful; she just needs more food and fewer drugs.

"I'll take you in the morning. You're not seeing that mother fucker again. He's a fucking loser, Lil. It's late, go to bed. We will talk in the morning and you will tell me everything."

"You can't tell me shit. I'll see him if I want. I don't owe you any explanation for anything. Why don't you leave? I don't need your help. So, thanks for coming by. It's been great seeing you again, but this little family reunion is over." She's oozing with sarcasm like she thinks I'll care and it will hurt my poor little feelings. It doesn't and I don't care.

Ignoring her attitude, I tell her again, "Go to fucking bed. I'm staying here tonight. We will talk in the morning. Don't test me, Lil. I'm very close to losing my shit again." Hoping the threat gets her to do what I'm asking.

"You're a fucking psychopath, you know that? I don't give a shit. I'm tired, anyway. Stay on the couch. Sleep on the floor, I don't care. You do you. And I will see Luke whenever the fuck I want. You're not my dad." She gives me the finger and walks away.

Yeah, ok and I'm the psychopath? Bitch, fuck you too. I take another drag of my smoke before putting it in one of the takeout bins littered before me.

We will be correcting that attitude real fast. I won't put up with her shit or anyone else's.

I'm starving, I haven't eaten since lunch. Getting up, I go to the kitchen and check out the food situation. Opening the cupboards, there is nothing but some instant noodle containers. Fuck that, nope, I need more substance than that. Hitting up the fridge next, it's bare. A few condiment containers on the shelf and some milk. That's it. No wonder she looks so fucking caved in, living off instant noodles, take out, plus the drugs explain it all.

Fuck it, I'm not eating tonight.

Tomorrow I'll stop at the grocery store on the way back. I can't live like this while I'm here. Racking my fingers through my hair, I blow out a deep breath in frustration. This is a bigger cluster fuck than I had anticipated.

What in the fuck have I walked in to?

CHAPTER 8

LILY

"Wake the fuck up, Lil. I have to take you to the pharmacy before heading into work."

Why is he still here?

"Could you please fuck off, cousin? I'm sleeping. I have the worst fucking headache, and I don't feel like dealing deal with your macho man shit today." I yell back at him, then throw the covers over my head.

"Get up. You have five minutes. We need to get you the morning-after pill."

I can't afford that. I can't even afford food. So no, we don't need to get me that pill. I lied when I told him Luke would take me.

Suddenly, my blankets leave my body. Opening my eyes slightly and I can see Jaxson standing over me. His muscular tattooed arms crossed and his frown lines are visible. I wonder if this is the only mood he operates on: pissed off.

"I can't afford the pill. I won't be getting the pill. Thank you so much for caring. Please go away." This is a last ditch effort to politely get rid of him. But he doesn't move. Motherfucker. Is he thick in the skull too?

"Jax. Go. I don't know why you're even here. I don't know why you suddenly give a shit about me, considering the last time I saw you before yesterday was over a year ago. You can't save me. I don't want to be saved. So leave. I'm fine." I move my face into my pillow and scream. He makes me so fucking angry. Why won't he listen to me? I'm completely sober, which means I can feel every single emotion in my body. I hate it. Now that I have felt what it's like not to feel, I prefer that.

My heart is beating fast within my chest from the mixture of anger, frustration, and dread. My mind keeps repeating the same things, *'I hate you, go away. I hate you. I don't need you. Go away. I was meant to be alone.'*

I feel Jinx snuggle closer to me. He is always able to sense it when I'm about to break.

My body starts to tremble as my breathing gets more intense. The voices are getting louder in my head. Covering my ears with my hands in an effort to make it all stop and I scream again into the pillow. I need them to stop. Please, just stop.

Suddenly, I feel my body leaving my bed. I don't open my eyes. But tears that were building behind them are still able to escape. I don't stop holding my ears. Eliminating more of my senses. I hate this. What did I do for all this to happen?

Before I even realize where I am, I feel warm water spraying on me. I'm being placed on the shower floor.

"What are you doing?" Opening my eyes and seeing Jax is in here with me. We are both soaked.

"You were having some sort of episode, Lil. I tried shaking you to get you to focus on my voice, but you were in a different fucking world. So I threw you in the shower."

"Go. I'm fine." whispering, as I try to catch my breath.

"Dry off. Get changed. We are going to the store. Then you can come back and mope around and be miserable."

"You're paying for it."

"Yeah, I figured as much. Now hurry the fuck up. I have to get to work." Leaving in a fit of rage. His soaked white shirt clinging to his muscular tattooed chest doesn't go unnoticed by me. Anxiety or not, I can always appreciate seeing that.

Getting up, I turn off the water that is still spraying

on me. Taking off my T-shirt and panties, I wrap myself up in a towel. Deciding that I can't last another second like this, I go straight to my medicine cabinet and grab the container of mixed pills, just the Xanax and Oxy that Luke left here for me and I decide today is a Xanax day. I toss it into my mouth and swallow it dry. This should kick in anytime and I'll be able to put up with my cousin's shit.

We got the magic pill. Stopped at a drive-thru for some breakfast and now he's dropping me back off at the trailer. We have spent most of this trip in silence. I love it. Him and his savior complex can get fucked. If I wanted help, I would ask. And I didn't fucking ask.

"I heard you can get crampy and shit after you take that pill, so don't be fucking stupid while I'm at work. I grabbed some Tylenol to help with cramping or whatever; it's in the bag as well. I'll be back later tonight."

"Whatever Jax." Is all I say as I get out of the truck with the bag.

Maybe I should slip him something when he's sleeping tonight. Maybe then he will get off my ass and chill the fuck out. He doesn't have a clue. He just barges in and tries to take over. I didn't ask for this. I didn't want any of this, and I'm sure as fuck not telling him anything about my life. I don't want his help, his sympathy, or his charity. I just need him gone.

Once inside, I put the bag on the counter and grab the pill box from inside of it. Without even reading the instructions or warnings, I open it up and take it, having no idea how I'll feel once it kicks in. So I walk over to the coffee table and roll a joint with the leftover weed still out. Lighting it, I bring it to my lips and inhale the sweet, stale smoke into my lungs. Holding my breath, seeing how long I can keep it in before my lungs try to cough. It doesn't take long until they try once, contract in my chest. I still don't let it out. Holding it there instead. My lungs contract again, begging to be freed, so I give in and exhale. I start coughing and my eyes water, but it's worth it. For that feeling. The glass of water from last night is still out. I take a sip to help calm down. This is all the pain management I need; weed, Xanax and the morning-after pill as today's special guest.

CHAPTER 9

LILY

Opening my eyes, I find myself still on the couch. Jinx is sleeping at my feet. He's the only one I trust and can rely on. That's the great thing with animals: they are loyal until the end. The world doesn't change them. They love unconditionally, and comfort you in times of need. No words spoken, they are just there for you. Humans aren't like this. The world influences us, greed and hatred make the headlines. People pick sides and contribute to the toxicity of society nowadays. And I don't want to subscribe to any of it.

Thanks to my cocktail, I feel a bit groggy from sleeping all day. If any side effects of taking the pill occurred, I am oblivious to it and my headache from earlier is completely gone.

Turning my head, I look for any sign of my pain in

the ass cousin. I hate that he thinks he can just barge into my life and bark orders at me. He has to be single. The man has zero people skills. He is hot. I won't take that away from him. Covered in tattoos, built and his eyes—one hazel, the other green. So unique. But that won't fool me. It won't blind me to his arrogance. He is no better than anyone else here. And walking in like he's running shit now. I barely know him.

I don't see his shoes or his miserable face glaring at me. Which means he's not here, so I'm going out tonight. Checking my phone, I have a few missed messages from Luke. One is checking in on me and another telling me to come to Ethan's tonight. So Luke is obviously not coming around here anytime soon after my cousin sucker punched him.

Jaxson had no right to do that to him. He had no right to ruin the most incredible high, sex, and feeling of raw passion between two people. I feel my anxiety rising just thinking about my frustrations with Jax. My mind doesn't shut off like most people's; it goes and thinks about the same situations repeatedly.

I get up from the couch and head to my room to change. Throwing on a pair of torn fishnet stockings, jean shorts and a black crop t-shirt with my black converse. Checking my appearance in the mirror, I touch up my black eyeliner, using my finger to smudge it around my eye and apply mascara, leaving my long black hair down. Then, I do a quick breath check, covering my mouth with my hand and blowing into it. Sniffing it, it's not good. Quickly heading to the bathroom, I brush my teeth and take one more quick look at myself in the mirror. Time to go before Jax shows up. He will want to talk and I'm not ready. I refuse to say what's happened in its entirety out loud. It will make it real. My parents left me to find themselves. My parents left me. I was not worth staying for. Not worthy of their love.There's no reason for people to stay with me. I will never be good enough.

Fuck. Stop thinking. I hate this. I need my brain to shut off before I get in too deep. Before leaving the bathroom, I decide this evening calls for an Oxy, so I grab one from the cabinet and swallow it down. This will shut it all off.

While waiting for it to kick in, I head out of the bathroom to find my cousin standing in the hallway, looking at me. Shit, I didn't even hear him come in.

"What the fuck is wrong with you? You can't just creep in here like this, you scared the shit out of me."

"Have you always been a bitch, or is this a part of the new Lily package you're offering?"

'Get fucked, Jax. I'm leaving and I suggest you do, too." Saying to him as I go to step around him.

"I don't think so. We have shit to discuss," he says, while reaching out to grab my arm in an effort to stop me. He is still in his work clothes and definitely needs a shower. He is filthy, with dirt and dust clinging to his exposed skin.

"Don't touch me," I shout, while glaring at him.

"I will touch you whenever I want, however I want, wherever I want."

I ignore his declaration.

"I am not discussing shit with you. You are wasting your time and breath on this. You won't get a word out of me."

"I will get a word out of you, one way or another, Lily. I am persistent. Don't expect me to give up easily, no matter how much of a bitch you are. You don't scare me."

"It won't work, but good luck, Jax. I'm leaving now. You do you, boo." I try moving around him again, but he still doesn't move out of my way.

"I bought groceries. When was the last time you had a meal other than instant noodles? You look like shit, way too thin, and you need to eat."

"I suppose you want me to say thank you? I don't need your charity, Jaxson. Now let me the fuck go." Now I'm getting pissed off. I just want to leave.

He steps closer to me, leaning in close, placing his dirty hands on my shoulders and whispers, "Show some fucking respect. Now, go to your room while I make some food. We will talk when I say we will talk.

You will come and eat when I say you come and eat. You can't hide from me."

I shake him off and just stare at him. Glaring into his eyes, fucking try me Jax, I dare you.

"Jinx, come here, boy." I call out before stepping back and shaking Jax's hold off me.

"I'm going into my room because I want to and I can't stand to be around you another minute. Not because you told me to." I am seething. The urge to punch him in the face is strong. I have never felt violent toward another person–until now.

Turning around before I do something I regret, I find Jinx at my feet, and I go into my room, closing the door softly. I will not give him the satisfaction of knowing he's gotten to me.

Jinx jumps on my bed, making himself comfortable in a ball.

Jaxson thinks he has won, but he hasn't. So when he comes looking for me, I won't be here.

I wait until I hear his footsteps start going down the hall towards the kitchen, and spring into action.

Did he want a round of applause for buying food? For pointing out that I can't afford more than instant noodles? Son of a bitch.

How fucking dare he.

I slowly start to slide my bedroom window open, not needing him to hear it. Inch by inch, I move it until it's fully opened. Next, I carefully and slowly pull out the screen so I can slide through it. Once it's entirely out, I put it on the floor. "Shh, Jinx. I'll be back." I say before lifting myself up on the window ledge and begin to move my body through, putting one leg through the opening and moving my upper body to the other side of the window. Repositioning my hands and bringing my other leg over, I jump down to the ground. I reach up and slide the window close as best I can without being too noisy.

I did it! I'm out. I run behind the trailer and take the back way through the bushes to Ethan's. There isn't any loud music playing, noticing as I get closer, so there must not be a party tonight. Just a chill sesh.

Running up his front stairs, I reach the door and turn the knob. It's unlocked, so I head in without knocking. Opening the door, I see Luke and Ethan on the living room couch, smoking a joint.

"Hey sweetness, come here. We've been wondering when you would come by," Ethan says, blowing out a cloud of smoke.

"Sorry, my cousin is over again. He is really starting to piss me off." I sigh as I make my way to the couch and sit between Ethan and Luke,

"Hey Lil, here want some?" Luke says, passing me the joint. He has a black eye and swollen nose from where Jax hit him. Fuck, I feel so bad. I take the joint from Luke's hand and hold it up to my lips. Taking a deep inhale, I feel the smoke fill my lungs, then slowly exhale, savoring every moment of it.

"Hmm, this is smooth. Is this new?" I ask, not remembering having this before. It doesn't taste like the others I have smoked with them.

"Yeah sweetness, a new blend we are trying out. Do you like it?" Ethan questions.

"I do. It's so smooth going down. And it's a chill out high, I really like it. Definitely need this more often." I tell him as I take another hit.

"You got it, sweetness."

"Lil, I got some other stuff I thought we could try tonight. What do you say, babe?" Luke says with a mischievous smile on his face. He is so handsome even with a busted face.

"What do you got Luke? Lay it on me." Smiling back at him.

With that, he reaches into his pocket and pulls out a baggy full of a white powdery substance.

"Cocaine, babe." He is dangling it in front of us.

I see Ethan move to the edge of the couch as I take another hit of the joint. He has a rolled up dollar bill in his hand.

"Luke, cut us some lines, man."

"Lil, watch Ethan and how he does it. Then do

what he does, ok? It may burn a bit, but it should be fine once you get used to it," Luke reassures me.

Nodding as I watch him open the baggy, take the corner of a card he got out of his wallet, gather some of the powder onto it, and bring it to the table.

Tapping the card on the table, he gets all the powder off it and starts moving it back and forth. Then he divides the cocaine into three equal thin lines.

Ethan leans forward, placing the rolled bill up to one nostril, plugs the other with his finger and snorts the line quickly up his nose. "Dude, she's going to love this," he says as he passes me the rolled bill.

I lean down and do what Ethan did. Placing the bill up my nose, I plug my other nostril and start to snort the line quickly.

My eyes water: this shit burns. I give Luke the bill and sniffle. The burn makes my nose feel like it's running. My eyes are still watering, and I wipe them with my hand.

"You weren't joking when you said it burns!"

"Yeah, babe, this stuff is the real deal. That's how you know it's going to work. It gets easier each time." Luke reassures me and then takes his line. He went quickly and seamlessly, like Ethan. Bastards are experts.

"Guys, I took an Oxy before I came over. How does that mix with the coke?"

"Oh shit, sweetness, you are about to feel a high

that's completely on another level. They call it a speed-ball. Maybe we should join you, so you aren't alone?" Ethan offers.

"Um, what's a speedball?" I honestly have no idea.

"Babe, when you mix something like Oxy with cocaine. An upper and a downer. Big time druggies will use heroin instead of Oxy. You will feel a rush which should hit anytime now, then come down and feel a calm, relaxing feeling." Luke explains as Ethan passes him a pill. They both take one.

"Alright, guys, hold on for the ride. This shit is about to get fun," Ethan says, laughing.

"Lil, we should fuck during the rush. See what it's like." Luke suggests. I like this idea. So I lean into him and start to kiss him as I feel my body begin to tingle from the drugs. Moving one leg to go over his legs and sit on his lap to get comfortable. I'm starting to feel the rush they explained. My heart is racing. The faster it goes, the more I try to match the beat when I kiss Luke. Quick kisses, with my pelvis grinding against his hardening cock. I feel it getting harder with each pass over it. Moaning into his mouth, he bites on my lip, pulling it and not letting it go. I like the slight pain it brings, causing me to moan again.

"Sweetness, those moans are killing me over here." Ethan groans, causing me to giggle.

Luke lets go of my lip and kisses me again before

leaning back to turn his head toward his friend. I look as well out of curiosity while looping my arms around his neck.

Ethan is in sweatpants, and you can see his erection pressing against the gray fabric.

"Hmm, Lil, maybe you should help Ethan out first." Luke suggests.

The idea of being shared by them makes my mouth water. I get off Luke's lap and move my way to the ground. Slowly, I crawl toward Ethan. He is already lowering his sweatpants and underwear when his cock springs free. Without even being that close to him, I can tell it is bigger than Luke's. Parting his legs wide as I reach him, I move closer and kneel in front of him.

"Hi sweetness, I've been waiting for this. You are so gorgeous," he compliments me and smiles. I like it. It makes me feel desired.

Smiling back at him, I get shy and nod.

"Aw Lil, you don't need to be shy with us," he reassures me as I move forward, licking my lips before gripping his hard length at the base with my tiny hands.

I take my tongue and slowly slide it from his base all the way to the tip, which causes him to shiver slightly as I go over his head. Then, precum starts to leak out of it, and I brush my tongue over it to get a taste.

Looking up at Ethan, I wrap my lips around his shaft.

"Fuck, Sweetness, you are so pretty like this. On your knees for me, sucking my cock. Fucking gorgeous."

Slowly taking him deeper in my mouth, I hollow my cheeks, and continue working with him. I need to feel him hit the back of my throat. To choke me with his cock so I can't breathe until he lets me. To black out from a lack of oxygen hitting my brain and lungs. I crave this kind of rush now. It brings me to the verge of thinking I could die, just to be brought back to life. I get lost in my thoughts and don't even realize it when I feel a body behind me.

"Keep sucking him babe, I can't sit there and watch you any longer. I need to be inside of your sweet pussy." Luke says as he starts to pull my shorts down my thighs to my knees.

"Luke, make our girl feel good. She is doing such a good job. Take me deeper, sweetness, you can do it." Ethan encourages. He moves one of his hands to the back of my head and pushes me further down his hard length. I gag on him, but still I need more.

Luke pulls down my fishnets next and then panties to join my shorts as I hear a wrapper tear from behind me. He is using a condom this time.

I feel his fingers move to my already soaked pussy.

"Oh, babe, you are already so wet for me," he whispers into my ear.

I moan as I feel him line his cock up to my entrance. He grabs onto my hips and slams into me. This feels surreal. I continue to work Ethan in my mouth as Luke works me with each hip thrust.

"Fuck sweetness, I'm going to cum and you are going to take every last drop," he sighs as his climax begins and his cock swells in my mouth about to explode.

Luke is still working me from behind. "Baby, you are so tight. You take me so well, I'm not sure how much longer I can last." Luke says, panting.

Then I feel Ethan's cum shooting into the back of my throat. He holds my head down in place as he works through his orgasm. I hear low moans escaping his mouth throughout. As it starts to die down, he lets go of my head, and I am able to slowly clean him off with my mouth. My lips make their way up his shaft with my tongue, licking him along the way. Not wanting to waste a drop, I suck on his head once more before removing his now semi-hard cock from my mouth, then licking my lips and looking up at him with pride.

"Sweetness, you did so good, so fucking good. Now let Luke take care of you, ok?" Ethan says with hooded eyes. I rest my head on the top of his thigh while bracing myself by placing one hand on the floor and let Luke fuck me from behind.

This is a night I will never forget.

A moan escapes me, and I know we need to do this again. Luke is incredible. The sex we have is incredible. He fucks me hard and fast, never stopping until we both have cum.

"Luke, keep going. Right there, don't stop please," I whimper.

"You never have to worry about that. I'm never stopping, babe," he states confidently as he continues to pound into me.

I start to feel the tingling going down my back. I'm not going to last much longer. That's when it hits, and my body starts to tremble as his cock works the spot inside of me.

"That's it, babe, cum all over my cock." He encourages.

My pussy clenches as he continues to fuck me, gripping his hard cock like a vise. I never want this feeling to end.

"Fuck yeah, babe, grip me like that. Milk my cock with your pussy, just like that." Luke moves even faster as he rides out his own orgasm, grunting between each thrust. Once his has subsided, he leans over and rests his head on my back, both of us breathing heavily and with him still inside of me.

"That was amazing. We have to do that again." I say breathlessly, while my heart races. Ethan immediately speaks up, "Oh definitely, sweetness, but next time I take that pussy, and he claims your ass." I nod in agreement. I have never tried anal before, The idea of both of them inside of me at once excites me. We are all so dazed between the drugs and sex that we don't even hear the front door open. All of a sudden I hear Jaxson's thunderous voice hollering, "You motherfuckers!" And the smashing of glass follows.

We are fucked.

CHAPTER 10

JAX

O f course, she wouldn't listen to a simple
instruction.

After I put the groceries away, I went
looking for her, but she was gone. I knew immediately
where she'd gone. That fucker Luke has a hold over
her. Not knowing where he lives in the park, I went
over to the neighbors and asked. Janice advised me he
would be at Ethan's, a couple of trailers down. She tells
me she's noticed Lily hanging out with them more in
the last month, which worried her. I asked why, in my
most convincing innocent and polite demeanor. When
she explained Ethan was the resident park drug dealer,
I thought my head was about to explode. Being the
upstanding citizen that I am, I thanked Janice for her
time and head over there, not letting on to how fucked

those two will be once I get there. Then, walking a few steps from Janice's front door to my truck, I grabbed the wooden bat from my truck bed, and walked over to Ethan's.

What I did not expect was to walk into what I did. These two fuckfaces are dead. The bald tool's dick was still inside of her, as her head rested next to the other fucker's small, soft dick. I could feel my face filling with rage the longer I took in the scene. They hadn't heard me walk in. "You motherfuckers!" I shout, while walking towards the glass coffee table and smash it with the wooden bat. It immediately shatters when I connect with it, causing them to finally react and start moving.

Lily sits up, which causes the one to fall back to the ground. I look down at him and see he wore a condom this time—thank fuck. The other one stands up from the couch, pulls his pants up, and starts approaching me. I hold my bat out in front of me. "Ah, I don't think so. Take one more step from where you are and I'll bash your fucking head in."

I am not fucking around here.

"Lil, it's time to come home. Seems like you've mistaken your room with this fucker's living room," I say to her without my eyes leaving the tall one. My bat is still out, and he stands there, not moving. From the corner of my eye, though, I see the tool on the ground start to stand up. I don't think so. So, I take my bat and swing it at his ribs. As it connects, a few loud cracking sounds fill the room. "Sit your ass down and stay there. I am here for Lily. Once I have her, we will leave and you will never see her again. You will never speak to her again and you will never come around her again." I could kill them.

"You can have her, bro. The bitch isn't worth it." The one still standing declares.

Did he really just say that to me?

She is worth everything.

Dropping the bat at my feet, I step in front of him, as though I am about to call a truce. Put him at ease before I beat the living shit out of him for what he just said about her. Reaching my hand out, "Yeah man, I get it." He goes to grab it and I move it quickly out of the way and punch him in the face instead.

I hold on to his shirt with the other hand to keep him in place and continue to beat his face. This motherfucker will regret his words.

"She is not just some bitch. You never speak about her like that again. You will never utter her name out of your mouth again. If I find out you have even looked at her or thought about her, I will come back here and only one person will be walking away alive, and it won't be you." Yelling between punches. He tries to fight back and a couple of shots connect with my ribs, but I have the upper hand on him, still being stronger and bigger than he is.

"Jaxson, stop. Stop Jaxson!" I hear Lily pleading with me. Instantly, I listen to her, lifting both my hands in the air and stepping back. Bending down, I grab the bat and turn my head to make eye contact with her. I need her to understand every word I am about to say. "Lily, I'll stop. But I meant what I said. I will kill them. I am not fucking around when it comes to you."

She looks at me momentarily, absorbing what I just said when she speaks up, sounding defensive. "Can we just go, Jax? This is embarrassing. I want you gone once I get back to the trailer, too. I don't need you. Stay the fuck away from me. You are ruining everything!"

"Are you serious right now? I'm all you got right now. These two morons don't give a fuck about you. You are nothing more than a plaything to them. Wake the fuck up, Lil. Can't you see this?"

"How fucking dare you? I'm done. Also, this. Right here? Right now? It's what we do. We use each other to get what we need. So yes, I am very much awake and see everything for what it is now."

It's the last thing she shouts at me before walking out of this fucks trailer. Dammit.

Looking at the two dip shits, "Stay the fuck away from her. Don't contact her. Don't come over. Walk the other way if you see her. This, whatever it was, is done. Stay away from Lily."

With my bat in hand and my point made clear, I follow after Lily. We are far from through. She can be mad at me all she wants right now, but one day she will look back and see I was doing the right thing for her.

Once I leave the fucker's trailer, I beeline it back to hers.

She's going to learn quickly. I won't put up with her attitude or druggie ass anymore. This show she's putting on is done.

I walk up the front stairs and head inside, shocked to see her sitting on the couch. I thought she would have tried to lock herself in her room to escape me.

Dropping the bat, and walking towards her. "Your pupils are pinned. I know you're on something. What did you take?"

She doesn't answer me.

"Lily, is that what you meant? Using each other? They fuck your holes, and in return you get high? Is that the trade-off? Are you a whore now, Lil?"

This gets a response out of her. She's on her feet

and in my face within seconds, pointing her finger against my chest.

"You have no fucking idea. No idea what I deal with on a daily basis. No idea what shit has been piled on me in the last month. Yeah, I am high. So. Fucking. High. It's the best I've felt in forever. Maybe the stick in your ass would disappear if you tried it."

She is such a bitch. I brush it off, though. This is about her, not me. She's just lashing out because I cut off her drug supply.

"So, I was right. You fuck them for drugs. Jesus Christ."

"Oh, don't judge me. You beat the shit out of people for looking at you the wrong way. You are just as fucked up as I am. My dad's told me stories about you. It's in our DNA. We aren't right up here, Jaxson." She says while tapping her head with her finger.

"This isn't about me. This is about you: stop trying to turn this around. What are you on? Tell me, for fuck's sake." Goddamnit, this girl is frustrating.

"Right now? It's weed and Oxy, with a hint of coke. This morning included a Xanax and the morning-after pill, but I slept it off. Did you know that mixing Oxy and coke is called a 'speedball'?"

"A fucking speedball! Do you know how dangerous that is? Oh, my fucking god. You aren't dumb, Lily, but you sure as fuck are acting it. Do you not see how thin you are? And not in a good way? School, tell me when was the last time you went?"

She is pointing her finger in my face now, and we are only inches apart. I think I've hit a nerve. But if this gets more information from her, I don't care. "You don't know shit. Nothing. My parents left me. Is that what you want to hear? They fucking left me. So I've decided to take my life into my own hands. I am all I got and all I need. This is the best I've ever felt in my entire life. My anxiety is gone. I'm finally free!"

"It's not gone, your anxiety. You're numbing it with drugs! You're fucking drug dealers for the drugs you use to numb it." Firing back at her.

She looks at me, not denying it. Then starts to walk away. I don't fucking think so. You are not running away from this conversation, cousin.

"I am not leaving." I yell at her. She needs to understand, running away from this won't make me disappear.

As she tries to pass me, I grab her arm, so she can't get any further.

Then, stepping closer to her, close enough that my body almost touches hers, I whisper into her ear, "If you like being a whore so much, you'll be my whore. Only mine. The only difference is, I won't give you drugs in exchange. Instead, you will get food, lot fees paid for the trailer and bills handled until I feel like you're ok enough to be left alone here. Until then, I am not leaving."

Looking back at me, she spits. "You disgust me."

"Good." Is all I say back as I let her go. She storms off to the bathroom and slams the door.

This girl needs to learn some fucking manners.

CHAPTER 11

LILY

I hate him. I hate him more than I hate my parents for leaving me. I hate that he had me admit it. That they left me. I hate him for caring. For wanting to try and save me. I don't want to be saved. I don't *need* to be saved. And I'm not a whore. I will never be his whore. So what if I like fucking, getting high and numbing my feeling? That doesn't make me a whore. It makes me a goddamn survivor in this world. Everything seems so loud. From the thoughts running through my head to the silence that surrounds me in the bathroom. Covering my ears won't make it stop. I'm leaning against the bathroom door, then decide to check my pill supply. Opening the cabinet, and seeing through the clear blue plastic bottle to find I only have two pills left from what Luke left me. Shit. I will need to figure out how to get more tomorrow. After Jaxson beat the shit out of both of them and destroyed Ethan's living room, I'm sure they will be in no rush to supply me.

I'm not ready to leave the bathroom yet. I'm not a coward, but if I have to listen to Jax for another minute, I will lose my fucking mind more than I already have. The need to submerge myself to further block everything out overwhelms me. Turning to face the bath, I lean over its ledge, and begin to draw a bath. As the water starts to fill, I begin to take off my clothes. Removing each item until I am fully naked, and they are in a pile on the floor at my feet. I step forward to get into the bath; the water is almost filled when I catch a glimpse of myself in the mirror. I see myself in the mirror every day, looking back at me each time. But now... I don't know. Looking around my eyes, they don't seem caved in, I am just tired. I am always so tired. Moving the gaze of my eyes down, I scan them over my body, the body he claims to be too thin. Is that even a thing? I mean, I don't think it's that bad. It's not like you can see my ribs or hip bones. Sure, I could stand to gain a few pounds, but I don't see what he is seeing.

Fuck. Stop. Brain, just stop, please. I am ok. I shake my head, to try and rid it of the shit my cousin said, and climb into the bath and turn off the taps. The water is so high once I sit down, it sloshes over the edge. I sit in it and lean against the back of the tub. This feels so good, the warm water against my skin. The only thing that would make this better is if I had a joint to enjoy while sitting here, but I didn't grab one in my rush to get away from Jax. I just had to get away from him. Closing my eyes, I start to focus only on my breathing. With each inhale and exhale, I feel myself relaxing more, my body no longer holding itself up, and I slowly start to become submerged under water. I feel the water rise, inch by inch, against my skin. Moving up my neck, then over my chin, past my ears, and finally over my head. I lay under the water, holding my breath with closed eyes. Embracing the complete silence, finally. I allow myself to enjoy it for a few moments until I start to feel my lungs contract from running out of air. Before I decide if I want to come up from underneath, I scream. Only I know I am scream-ing. The water silences the sound of the outside world. I give it all I have, until the very last bit of air leaves me and causes me to sit up, bringing my head out of the water. I open my eyes, sitting for a moment without moving. The noises are gone. It's finally quiet again.

It's the following day when a loud noise from the kitchen wakes me. That motherfucker is still here. I get up, not bothering to change. I am in my underwear and a plain black sleep shirt. Walking out of my room, I drag myself down the short hallway and find him standing in the kitchen. "Good, you're up."

I don't respond. Instead, remembering he bought groceries the other night, and turn to the fridge, opening it to see what I can find. It's too early to deal with his voice, his words, his presence. Shit, I have not seen the fridge this full in what feels like ever. We didn't have a lot, but we got by. Feeling overwhelmed by all the choices, I grab the jug of orange juice and close the fridge door. Turning around, I walk toward the cabinet that holds the cups, but before I can make it all the way there, Jaxson steps in front of me. Without saying a word, he takes the orange juice container from my hand and sits it on the counter behind him. I look at him, confused as fuck. "What are you doing?" My voice is still gravelly from still not being fully awake.

"Go back to the fridge."

The guy is fucking insane. But it's too early to argue with him, so I walk a couple of steps back to the fridge.

"Ok, now what? If you expect me to fetch your breakfast, you will be disappointed."

"On your knees and crawl to me, pet," he demands.

Has he lost his mind?

"Are you sure you aren't high? I'm not doing that."

"I told you last night; you want to eat? Do you want this roof over your head? Do you want to be a whore? I'll give you all of that, so if I say get on your knees and crawl to me, you'll get on your knees and crawl to me. Without question. Do you understand, pet?"

I am speechless. This can't be real. I still haven't moved when Jax starts talking again. "Also, I went through the house last night after you went to your room. All the drugs are gone. The bottle of pills in the bathroom and the random pills on the coffee table have been flushed. You can keep the weed. It will help with your anxiety, but no more of that other shit, Lily. If you have anything in your room stashed, pass it over. If I find it later, there will be punishments."

"You can't do this. You can't just barge in here like you own the fucking place and throw my shit away and make rules that suit your needs. This is my fucking trailer." I yell at him, as I feel myself start to panic. Tears are pooling in my eyes; he threw it all away. How am I supposed to handle this?

"Lil, focus on my voice. Let me distract you. It will go away. Just focus on me." He encourages.

"On your knees and crawl to me. You're my own personal whore now, pet."

Not thinking, I get to my hands and knees on the kitchen floor and begin to crawl the short distance toward him. He puts his hand on my head, "Good job, pet. Now pull my pants down and suck my cock. And before you even think about it, if you bite me, I will have no issue punishing you for being bad. I don't want to have to do that, but if you do anything you aren't supposed to, you'll give me no choice. Do you understand?" He says in a tone I have not heard from him before. He sounds like Jaxson, but how he explains everything is like another side of him I am not familiar with. Caring and compassionate. But I feel oddly comforted sitting before him like this with his hand now rubbing the top of my head. I close my eyes and just focus on his hand, slowly rubbing the top of my head and the sound of his fingers against my hair. My chest slows and my breathing normalizes.

"Good job, pet. Now do what I said. Pull my pants down and suck my cock before I have to go to work. You are my whore now, only mine. I have no issues punishing you, so you learn for next time. Don't try anything stupid. Nod if you understand."

And Jaxson Reed is back. Fucking prick.

As I begin to undo his pants and unzip the zipper,

I nod. Then, moving his shirt up slightly, I brush my fingers over his hard tattooed abs as I go to pull his pants down.

He is already hard. The outline of his hard cock pressing against the fabric. I tilt my head up at him briefly and see he is watching me; he raises his eyebrows to tell me to continue. My cousin is enjoying this far too much, bastard. Moving my gaze slowly down his body, you can tell he is fit as fuck even when wearing his t-shirt. I pull his pants down his legs until they hit the ground. Then, grabbing the elastic waistband of his boxers I begin removing those next. His hard cock springs out. There is a shiny silver bar going through the tip, which also has precum starting to drip from it. Fuck me, it's gorgeous. He has a tattoo of a sword on his pelvis, it's in the same black and gray ink just like the rest of his body art. And that fucking delicious V line guys get, the arrow pointing us in the right direction. I move my gaze back down, and he's big, bigger than Ethan and Luke. Feeling slightly intimidated and excited, I bite my lower lip.

"You can do it, pet," Jaxson encourages as he grips his cock and begins to move his tip along my lips.

Unable to resist, I stick my tongue out and lick his head. The salty taste of his precum erupts on my tongue. I immediately go in for more. Wrapping my lips around his cock, I take him in my mouth and grip him with my hands at his base. Starting off by playing with his sensitive head, moving my tongue along his slit a few times to get him worked up; teasing him perfectly. I feel his hand on the top of my head again; this time his fingers are gripping my hair as he grunts. "Just like that. You are doing so good. Now, take all of me." He thrusts himself all the way into my mouth and slides down my throat. I close my eyes and as he begins to face fuck me.

I like how rough he is. He doesn't hold back or take it easy on me. He knows I am not some delicate flower, he clearly senses that.

"Open your eyes, keep them on me, pet." He demands. Listening, like the good pet I am, I look up at him through each thrust he makes, working himself in my mouth. I feel his head swell, "You will drink every last drop," and I moan in agreement. His breathing picks up as his release builds, his movements get faster and his hold on my hair tightens to keep me in place. I have to hold on to his muscular legs for support.

"Fuck, you are doing so good. Your mouth feels so good on my cock," he moans. That's when I feel his cock swell and ribbons of his warm cum hit the back of my throat. He continues his hard thrusting as his orgasm goes on, never letting up.

As it starts to die down, his pace slows until he is satisfied all of his release has coated my throat and then stops. Jax lets go of my hair, and I slowly start to slide my mouth off his dick. But, before fully removing himself, I suck his tip once more, being sure to get every last drop and clean his piercing off and then let go of his legs.

After looking at me for a few seconds, he kneels down with his pants still down and his now softening dick hanging out. Reaching for my face, he places both hands to hold my face and leans in to kiss me. It's a soft kiss, not at all aggressive like I thought it would be. I feel his tongue at my lips, and I part them so he can enter, and we immediately deepen it. It's like he is sucking the air right out of my lungs. This kiss is different from any other I have had before. His lips are so soft, he is being so delicate with me. I wonder if he can taste himself on my tongue?

We stay kissing for what feels like a few more minutes, but it was probably only seconds when he inches away, and whispers, "You may have your orange juice now, pet, and make sure you eat some food with it. I need you to gain some weight for me, ok." Then stands as he pulls up his pants.

Once they are done up, he steps around me, as I am still sitting on the floor processing what the hell just happened. I don't fully comprehend it yet.

"My cell number is on the fridge, call me. Any reason, any time and I will answer. I should be back around eight." He yells before grabbing his tool belt off the floor that is at the front door and heads out.

I hate him.

CHAPTER 12

LILY

The asshole got rid of everything. He wasn't joking, thinking as I close the medicine cabinet. My Oxy and Xanax are gone; the couple of Ecstasy that Luke left here the other night are also gone. All Jaxson left me with was the weed. How am I supposed to get through the fucking day without them? I hated how it was before them. My hands start shaking when panicked thoughts enter my mind. Checking my phone, I don't have a single notification, nothing from Luke. It's mid-day, he usually has sent something to me by now. Fuck.

Fuck my cousin. Fuck him. He fucked it all up for me last night. We were enjoying ourselves. Everything was consensual. "Goddammit!" I yell into the air as I bang my fists against the bathroom countertop. Everything was fine before he barged in and inserted himself into my life. I feel tears start to trickle down my cheek out of pure frustration. I didn't even know I was crying until then.

I start my breathing exercises. I am feeling too much. My entire body is overcome by this fucking anxiety. I continue to focus on my breath. Closing my eyes, I bring my hands to my chest and feel my heartbeat while just concentrating on the rhythm of it. This helps me cancel the voices that my thoughts tell me, *'you won't make it without the pills. No one will love you again'.*

Fuck this. I'm going to Ethan's. Maybe they are too scared to text me in case my cousin sees it come in on my phone. Plus, I need to do some damage control, and I need my pills.

I've been knocking on Ethan's door for the last twenty minutes. He is home. His car is in the driveway. Luke is absolutely in there with him. "Answer the door. It's just me. Jaxson is at work." I plead now with each knock. "Please. I didn't even do anything. It was all my cousin. Please, just please, help me." I am begging now. I sound so fucking pathetic, and I feel it even more. This is so fucking embarrassing. When did I become this girl?

"Sorry, babe, your cousin fucked this up for you. You're on your own; you won't be getting shit from us anymore." I hear Luke yell through the door. Fucking pussy drug dealers.

"Fuck you guys. I'll just find someone else." I shout back.

I don't know anyone else. Finally, the reality of the situation hits me. My eyes start to well with tears again.

I have no one left.

I walked around the trailer park after leaving Ethan and Luke. Hoping the fresh air would help me feel better. Instead, it only caused me to try and further understand how I got into this situation. Was I that bad that my parents had no other choice but to leave me? I know what the letter said having read it a million times. My over analyzing of it, is doing nothing. It always comes back to the same thoughts: what did I do? What could I have done better? I never caused trouble, never talked back and not once complained about where we lived or our financial situation. So why don't they want me anymore?

I'm back home now, sitting on the couch, eating chips I found in the cupboard and smoking a joint. The walk and the silence of being outside got to me and my thoughts are still circulating in my brain. Yeah, my cousin is here, but eventually, he will leave too. I am just a whore for him to use, so I don't actually matter to him, anyway. But I want to matter to someone, anyone.

Why did he have to get rid of my pills? Fuck.

I have heard some aspects of weed helps with anxiety, and so far it is helping take the edge off a bit, I am definitely high. But nothing beats Xanax and Oxy. The pills last much longer and they completely numb me. I fucking love that feeling. It's no wonder people get addicted to that shit. It's the best feeling out there, the best feeling I may never get to experience again if Jaxson gets his way. Now I just want to hide. Stay in the dark and never be found. What is my purpose now?

Taking another hit, I hold it in for as long as my lungs can stand it before they start begging me for release. Something about being on the verge of blacking out excites me. Your lungs begging you to gasp for air, but you don't. It is a rush. I try to last longer every time. Counting in my head, one, two, three... at fifteen, I finally give in as my lungs begin to contract and blow out the smoke, and at that exact moment, Jax walks in. He looks exhausted, with bags under his eyes and dirt smudged over his face. He is toeing off his work boots, then looks at me, "Get the fuck off my bed and maybe smoke that in your own room."

Well, aren't we chipper?

"Hard day at work, cousin?" I ask while smirking.

"Yeah, it was. Everything that could go wrong did. I am fucking exhausted. I just want to shower, eat, then go to sleep. So get off my fucking bed and do whatever you are doing somewhere else."

I don't move other than to bring the joint back up to my lips to take another hit and blow out a cloud of smoke in his direction. I can play too, dear cousin.

"Oh, no thank you. I think I am comfortable right here. You can go home if this is such an inconvenience for you?"

This asshole is going to learn he doesn't control me. I can't even control myself.

And I know in the back of my mind, I need to push him away before he can do it back to me. I will not be left again.

CHAPTER 13

JAX

I'm exhausted. I just want to shower, eat and go to sleep. The couch I've been staying on hasn't been terrible, but the novelty has worn off. Now Lily is here testing my patience with her fucking theatrics.

"Just think, cousin, I stopped to get you more weed on my way home. This shit is supposed to help with anxiety and stress better than the shit you were getting off those assholes. Trust me, I tried theirs and it was garbage." I tell her as I drop the new bag on the coffee table before her. She takes the opportunity to blow another cloud of shit weed smoke in my face.

"Now pet, that wasn't very nice." I tsk at her.

I know exactly how I will teach my pet–my whore–a lesson.

Turning on my heel, I head back outside to my old

work pickup truck, not bothering to put my shoes back on. Reaching the bed of the truck, I open my toolbox in the back and rummage around it until I find both of the things I need to teach my pet that her bad manners will not be tolerated. It takes me a few minutes, but I got it. Closing my toolbox, I shove my supplies into my pocket before going back inside, and she is right where I left her. Sitting on the couch, or my bed for the time being, smoking her joint. Walking towards her after closing the door behind me, she blows another cloud of smoke at me. Oh pet, you really shouldn't have done that.

"Give me the joint. I need a hit after the day I've had," I say while holding out my hand. There is barely anything left, but she passes it to me. Bringing it to my lips I suck it in, then put the remainder in an empty bottle on the coffee table. At the same time, I lean over, grab the back of her head and bring her mouth up to mine. Our lips are touching when I part mine and blow the smoke out from my mouth to hers, then I pull back from her.

Her guard is down. She inhales it while looking me in the eye. My eyes are different. Each a different color, it's always the first thing people notice about me. I'm sick of hearing about them, to be honest. I have my entire life and it annoys the shit out of me now.

While I have her focus on me, I grab both her

wrists with my hands and bring them over her head. Using my knee, I tap her leg and encourage her to move and lie on the couch. She does while blowing out the last bit left from what I gave her. Then, I straddle one leg over her so I am sitting on top of her. Lily starts biting her lip as she continues to watch me.

This girl has no fucking has no idea.

I can hold on to her wrists with one hand. She is so tiny and frail. Fuck, I need to get her to eat more, but I will deal with that later. Lily has so many layers that need to be peeled back. First, I need to break her, then I'll help put her back together.

I use my other hand to lift her short shirt up so it's over her head and covering her face, it's for the best that she doesn't see this next part coming. Flipping the cup of her bra on the left side, it exposes her breast and hard nipple. I bet she's soaked, but that's not why this is happening. I move my finger over her nipple in circular motions to keep it hard. And to keep her from realizing what is really going on. Once I have played with it several times, I pinch it before letting go, causing her to moan.

It's time, reaching now into my pocket and grabbing the nail I found in my toolbox. It's a long, thin silver nail used for hanging a picture frame, perfect for what I am about to do. It's just the right length and sharpness for this. Holding the nail in my mouth and then grabbing the pliers next, I set the pliers next to my one leg on the couch, straddling her, and take the nail from my mouth and hold it between my thumb and forefinger.

"Now, pet, whatever you do, do not move. Do you understand?"

She nods her head from under her shirt.

"Words. I need your words, pet." I coax out of her.

"Yes. Yes I understand." she rasps.

Her chest is moving a bit faster. She's nervous and excited. If it moves any faster, I will know it's her anxiety and stop everything. I'm not a complete dick.

I watch it move up and down a few more times and decide it's safe to continue. Blowing on her nipple, making sure the cool air keeps it hard.

Working with only one hand, I will have to move quickly and with a lot of force behind it to ensure it gets all the way through.

On her next inhale, I move. Putting the weight of my hand on the outside of her breast, I line up the nail to the middle of the nipple and push it through in one swift movement. Her hips buck up at me where I am sitting on her, and she screams. Then, I grab the pliers and start to bend the sharp end of the nail into a hoop so it meets the blunt end. Blood is dripping down from where I did the piercing.

"Get off of me!" She screams at me. I don't listen.

Instead, I move my head down and place my tongue where the blood trail is starting and slowly start to lick it up from the bottom of her breast, slowly all the way up to the nipple. Sweet like nectar

Her blood is my blood. Our blood is addictive.

I need more.

I grab the switchblade on my belt that I always have when I am in my work gear and flip it open. Under Lily's breast, I put the tip of the sharp blade against her skin and push it so it creates another trail of blood. I throw the knife on the table and lap my tongue over the new stream. She has stopped fighting me, her breathing still heavy, but not too rapid. She's ok, so I put my lips over the knick I made and kiss it. Leaving her blood on my lips. I pull the shirt from over her face back down, still keeping hold of her wrists, and lean in and kiss her. We don't deepen it. Instead, Lil uses her teeth to nip at my lip. The last nip she does hurts and I know she's drawn blood. That's when we start to devour each other. The mixing of our blood, the taste of it entering our mouths and the flavor hitting our taste buds ignites a frenzy. I want to take this further, but won't. This was meant to teach my pet a lesson, not to be rewarded. Before I get carried away to the point of no return, I pull back and just look at her beautiful body. Taking every inch of her in before ending this moment.

"Keep it clean. You don't want it to get infected. You will not take it out. If you do, I will just do this all over again. I own you, now everyone will know."

"You are a fucking barbarian," she spits at me. Like I care.

"I told you I would punish you, pet, if you didn't behave. Consider this mild compared to what else I can do." I smile down at her and lick the last of our blood from my lips.

As I sit up, I let go of her wrists and grab my blade and pliers before walking down the hall to the bathroom. I feel my cock straining against my work pants. I need a cold fucking shower.

When I came out of the bathroom, the couch was empty and her bedroom door was closed. My shower was quick and very cold. That shit earlier made my dick hard. I thought about jerking off in the shower, but decided against it. I want her to have to handle it in the morning for me, and the wait will be worth it to see her lips around my dick. Just the thought makes me smile.

I made myself a sandwich for dinner. Something quick because I am exhausted. I have work in the morning, and I have to get up before the sun does. But before going to sleep, I want to play one more game with my pet. Standing up from the small kitchen table, I leave the plate on it. Wearing my gray sweats with my tattooed torso exposed makes me think of getting more ink put over-top of what is already there, with minimal room left on me for anything else, it would be the only option. I've seen others do it and it looks pretty cool. I also see Lil checking it out, so I know she also likes it. Maybe when she turns eighteen, I'll take her for her first one. First, she needs to get her shit sorted and finally tell me everything about her parents not being here. If she hasn't already, she will quickly learn I do not reward my pet for bad behavior.

Walking down the short hallway I stand in front of her bedroom door. There's no sound coming through the door, so she's either asleep or snuck out again. Taking hold of the door knob and slowly beginning to turn it so she doesn't hear me, I feel when the latch clicks, and I slowly start to open the door. The room is black, lit only by the moon in the night sky, peaking through the window. I open the door enough to get through it. The hinges squeak and I don't want her to wake up. Looking toward her bed, she is in it and her cat is sleeping in a ball at the end of the bed. Sorry buddy, but you're going to have to move. Leaving the door open behind me as I tiptoe to her bed, and leaving my sweatpants on as I lift her blanket slightly and slide into her double bed. This causes her to stir and I remain entirely still, hoping this hasn't woken her. She settles back down, laying on her side with her back to me. It's perfect for what I have planned. I turn as if to big spoon her, reach my arm around her waist and place my hand gently against her stomach. She is only wearing her panties and a t-shirt to bed. I begin to inch my fingers under her panty line and feel she is bare. My mouth instantly waters. This is the first time I am feeling her like this. I continue moving down until I feel her pussy. Taking one finger, I circle her lips before inserting one inside her. I find the spot I am looking for and begin rubbing it slowly. I don't want her to wake up yet, but I feel her starting to get wet on my finger. As I continue, I feel her hips begin to move slightly, and I stop immediately and whisper into her ear, "Don't move. Don't say a word or I will leave you dripping and needing more." Unsure if she is awake enough to hear or understand, I don't really care. She's been warned. Now it's up to her to decide if she will listen. I wait a moment before starting up again, ensuring she doesn't try to move again. Then, adding another finger inside her tight pussy, I begin to circle her swollen clit with my thumb. She is dripping down my fingers as I continue to work her.

"Such a good pet. Stay completely still." I rasp into her ear. My cock is strained against my pants, but I resist the urge to pull myself out and shove it deep inside of her. She is so beautiful like this, at my mercy, listening to my commands. I hear a moan slip out of her mouth, which causes me to stop again, "Now, pet, I just told you how good you were doing. Don't make me have to take that back."

"I'm sorry, keep going, please. I'll listen."

I begin moving again, her orgasm getting ready to move through her body as her pussy grips my fingers like a vise. I move them faster inside of her and against her clit. Her body trembles, but I don't stop. This feels too good, her release coating my fingers as I continue to work her through it. I pump my fingers in her two more times to draw the last bit out of her. Her breathing is heavy and her trembles have subsided. Removing my fingers from her now soaked panties, I bring them to my mouth and suck her delicious juices off them. She is mine. I own her entirely now.

She breaks the silence, still not moving. "I hate you."

"Good."

CHAPTER 14

LILY

"Get up, Lily. You need to eat before I head out." Jaxson yells from wherever the fuck he is in the trailer.

God damn it, I hate him.

Last night is still running wild in my head. What the hell is happening? He took whatever I had left, good or bad, away from me. Stole my last glimpse of happiness from my grasp. I miss the pills. I miss them so much. My brain doesn't stay still for long anymore, my emotions taking over. I am starting to feel more than I care to again. I don't want to have to confront how I am feeling. Before all this happened, my anxiety was not great, but nothing like this. My parents' leaving me triggered something, making everything so much worse. I guess abandonment will do that to a person.

My nipple is still throbbing. I can't believe he took a fucking nail to it. He cut me and licked my blood, but I bit him back and took his, too. I guess being fucked up likes company, and I definitely fed off his company last night.

Then later, when he snuck into my room and touched me while I slept. Forcing me to remain completely still and quiet. The amount of willpower it took was almost unbearable, but it also allowed me to just focus on the now. As much as all of this is insane, it is helping. Of course, I will never admit that to him. The fucker already has some kind of savior complex. No need to further encourage it or build up his already bloated ego.

"Lily. Up. NOW." Oh, someone is testy this morning. Maybe he should have slept instead of finger banging me last night.

"I'm up, asshole. Calm down." I shout back at him.

"Come on Jinx, up we go, let's get some breakfast," I say while yawning into my hand. What time is it anyway? The sun is barely starting to come up. Reaching over, I grab my phone and see it's only 5:30am.

What in the fuck.

I get up, make my way to the kitchen, and find him leaning against the counter with a coffee in his hand

and his shirtless, muscular, tattooed torso on display. He is in sweatpants, and his dark hair is a mess.

"Why in the fuck are you waking me up this early?" I'm really fucking annoyed.

"Now, pet, on your knees."

I don't move.

"Do you want to be taught another lesson? We can add a piercing to your other nipple."

Bastard.

I don't want another one, so I kneel and look at him. He puts his coffee down behind him on the countertop and walks toward me.

"I will give you money to get supplies from the drugstore to clean your newest addition. We don't want it getting infected, do we, pet? Are you my good little whore?"

"Yes, I am," I whisper. I don't need it to get infected. What would happen if it did? Will it fall off? Imagine explaining that to the doctor. *So Doc, my insane barbaric cousin decided I was being bad one night and stuck a nail through my nipple.* No, thank you to that awkward and uncomfortable conversation. I bet he would call the police or commit me.

"Good girl. Now stay where you are. Open your mouth, tongue out, and don't close your eyes. Always on me. Do you understand, pet?"

"Yes." Then I do exactly what he has asked.

He begins to pull his pants down, and he isn't wearing underwear. His pierced, hard cock bounces right out of them. Jaxson grips it with his tattooed hand, and I think he is about to force it down my throat, but instead, he surprises me. He begins to rub his tip with his thumb while looking at me with hooded eyes. Precum starts to leak out and his thumb rubs it into his skin. Then he begins to move his hand slowly up and down his shaft. Working himself in front of me. I want to lean forward and lick him. But I can't, I must listen. I concentrate on his movements, his hand moving up and down his hard length.

"Hmm, cousin. Do you like what you see? This is all for you. Only for you. I own you now. YOU. ARE. MINE." He growls.

To be wanted.

To be owned.

I find it strangely comforting. It almost gives me purpose again since my parents left.

His breathing picks up with each movement of his hand, his hips begin to buck and his tip swells. Then ropes of cum shoot out and land on my face. I keep my eyes open as his cum shoots at me, even though instinct tells me to close them. I focus on keeping them open for him. More of his warm release hits my face, some making it into my mouth and some above my brows. It begins dripping down and coats my eyelashes. The last bit releases from him, and he aims it to hit my tongue.

"Now swallow it, pet."

Without hesitation, I bring my tongue back in my mouth and swallow his release. Still, not moving from where I am sitting.

"Good job. Now clean me off." He demands.

I lean in and lap his tip with my tongue. Cleaning off any cum left and then wrap my lips around him to make sure I get everything, even getting his piercing clean. The feeling of the cold metal on my tongue mixed with this warm salty cum is my favorite.

My panties are getting wetter by the second. My cousin needs to leave so I can take care of myself next. Once I'm satisfied that I got it all, I pull back and look back up at him.

He pulls his sweats up, "Go clean yourself off and make sure you eat before going out today. Text me a picture of your meals. I want you to gain weight. You're still too thin, Lil. I need you to be healthy."

"Ok, Jaxson." I don't fight him. There's no point.

He steps toward me and rubs my head with his hand, and I lean into his leg. It immediately clears my mind. I am stuck in the moment. I'm not in my head for once and I'm finding this strangely comforting.

"Good girl. Now go clean up. I have to get changed and head to work."

I nudge against his leg more, still not understanding it, but this calms me. I stay leaning into it for another minute while he continues to rub my head before getting up and walking out of the kitchen to clean myself off.

CHAPTER 15

JAX

nother long fucking day at work. I like my job working in construction, but some days it's exhausting. It's already after nine and I am just pulling up to the trailer now. I just want one night where I get home and I don't have to deal with her bratty ass and hopefully, tonight is that night. I park my truck and get out, locking the door before grabbing my work belt from the truck bed and looking at the trailer.

Please let her be home.

Walking inside, the lights are on, but I don't see her. "Lil, you home?" I shout from the front door as I remove my boots and drop my tool belt next to them. I don't get a response from her and I swear if she is with those morons, I'll be in jail within the next hour. Fuck.

"Lily. Answer me. Are you home?"

From the corner of my eye, I see her cat come out from behind the coffee table. What the fuck? Jinx is never out here unless Lily is. He usually sticks to her bedroom. I walk over to where he is now sitting. Maybe he got a hold of something and is playing with it. Who knows. When I look down behind the coffee table, my heart stops. Lily is lying on the floor between the couch and table, curled in a tight ball, shaking. I instantly drop down next to her, brushing her fallen hair away from her face, "Lil, it's me." She doesn't respond, and I am not sure if she registers my presence.

Without hesitation, I scoop her up in my arms, sit on the floor, and just hold her against my chest. "Lil, talk to me. What happened?" I plead. I feel so helpless. Her body is still shaking, her breathing is rapid, and her eyes are tightly closed. Fuck. I swear to satan, if those assholes came here and did this to her, I will fucking end them for hurting her. For looking at her after I told them to stay the fuck away. I feel the rage swimming through my body, recognizing that if Lil feels it, it will only worsen things. I close my eyes and clear my head. Needing to just focus on her. She is my priority.

"Pet, please. Anything, tell me anything." I beg, as I continue to hold her close and rub her head. I noticed she likes it when I do this.

"I thought. I thought... it's late," Lily whispers.

I have no idea what she's talking about? What is late? Her period? I took her for the morning-after pill. There's no way she has that fucker's baby in her.

"What is late, pet?" closing my eyes, I lean back, and hope she doesn't say what I think she is going to.

"You. You were late. It's late. I thought. I thought you left me, too."

"I would never leave you. I am so sorry, pet. I should have called and told you I was running late. I am so sorry. So. Fucking. Sorry."

I am such an asshole.

"I hate feeling like this. You took it all and now I feel again. I hate it. I hate you. You made me like this. You made me care." Lily sobs.

She's fucking broken. I thought breaking her would feel better than this.

But, instead, I feel like shit.

I place her next to me on the floor. "Stay here. Let me fix this. Let me help you, pet." She doesn't respond. Just leans against the couch, holding her legs to her chest.

I sit up on the couch and lean forward, grabbing from my pocket the baggy of weed I took from here from last night, then a paper from next to it and begin rolling her a joint. Her attack is a mixture of her not having her pills– the pills she doesn't need–and me being a complete dipshit and not telling her I would be late. I know she got worked up over shit like this, and I completely overlooked it.

Once I finish rolling it, I seal it closed and light it. I take the first hit and hold it out in front of her. "Pet, please take this. This will help, I promise."

I see her faintly nod, then reach for it. Bringing it to her lips, she sucks it back. Like it's the first proper breath she has had in hours.

"That's it, Lil. You are doing so good. Now blow it out. Inhale, then exhale."

She follows my instructions, blowing it out like a weight has been lifted off her shoulders, then goes in for another.

"I am so sorry, Lil. I didn't think... I wasn't thinking. I should have called." I say softly and with absolute honesty.

Moving a little closer to her, I place my leg against her bent one, and start to rub her head again. She moves into me, adjusting her position. Her head leans against my leg and then wraps one arm around my calf.

"Tell me about your day before I fucked up. Did you go to the store and get what you needed, pet?"

She nods.

"Words. I need words."

With a shaky breath, "Yes, yes, I did. Thank you for leaving me money for that, Jaxson."

"Of course, anything for you. Always. Never, ever

doubt that. And I promise I will never do this again. I will always call or text if I'm running late. I swear it."

She doesn't respond. It's ok. I just need her to focus now on feeling better. These attacks must take so much out of her tiny body. She probably feels exhausted after. I hope she is able to pass out until morning once she is ready for bed.

Lily tries to pass me the joint, but I don't take it. "Pet, I need you to finish it all for me. Can you do that?"

"Yes." she whispers into my leg.

"You are doing so good. Just keep inhaling and exhaling. There is medicine in that. It will help calm your mind and body."

The CBD in it will help her more than those fucking pills she was popping.

We stay like this for a few more minutes while she finishes the joint. Once it's almost at the end, I put my hand out and she holds it out for me to take. I grip it and bring it to my mouth, taking the last hit before putting it out on the dish in front of me.

"Pet, are you hungry? Can I make you something?"

She shakes her head. "I can't eat when I get like this. My appetite doesn't exist," she explains.

I understand stress and anxiety can mess with your entire body like this.

"Can I take you to bed? You must be tired?"

She just nods against my leg again as I continue to rub her head.

I hate that she feels this way. It kills me, but I love that she finds comfort in me like this.

"Ok, let's get you off to bed then. You need to rest. You're exhausted. Are you ok if I carry you?"

"Yes, please, Jaxson. I just feel so tired."

With that, I stand up, and she lets go of my leg, then I sweep her up into my arms bridal style and start to walk to her room, and Jinx follows us.

This girl. I wish I could take her demons and protect her from all this pain. I'd give anything to take this burden away from her. There's nothing more I want than to see her thrive, to live without worry or fear.

Early the next morning, I'm up before the alarm on my phone goes off. We are both cramped into her small bed next to her fucking cat.

"Jinx, off. Now." I hiss at him.

He just looks at me, not moving. Fucker.

Moving my foot under the covers towards him startles him, and he jumps off. I have won this round cat. I need to make my pet feel good. She's had a rough

24 hours and needs this as much as I do. Maybe this will help make up for my epic fuck up last night. It took me ages to fall asleep after I put her to bed. Thankfully, she passed out immediately from exhaustion.

I hate that I was the cause of her pain. Thinking back on it just pisses me off. I would punch myself in the face if I could. Racking my fingers through my hair, I blow out a breath in an effort to calm down. I need to make this up to her.

Slowly moving my body further under the covers, I inch my way over to her. It doesn't take much effort with it being a double bed. My head is at her hips, and I don't want to wake her, but in order for me to get into position, I need to move the blankets slightly off of her.

I move myself between her legs, lay on my stomach, and take in the sweet scent of her covered pussy. Taking my forefinger, I move her panties to the side and hold them there. Moving my head up slightly, I bring my tongue out and lick between her folds. She moves her hips ever-so-slightly, but she still seems asleep. I do it once more before moving up to her clit, taking it between my lips and sucking on it. She wiggles again against my face and I stop, staying in place and waiting to see if this has woken her. I wait for a moment and when I see no change in her obedient body, I continue my assault on her pussy. Sucking her clit in my mouth and using my tongue to play with it as I bring my other hand's fingers up to her already wet lips and insert two fingers inside of her. Thrusting them against her g-spot, I begin to feel her clench around them.

"Fuck, keep doing that," Lily groans, causing me to smile with her demand.

Moving faster with my fingers causes her hips to buck and her hands that are under the covers, to grab onto my hair and push my head further into her pussy. My pet is grinding her pussy against my face as I continue to work her. Her orgasm is building, I can feel it with each movement. She is chasing it.

With one final suck of her clit, she starts to cum all over me. Her legs tremble next to me and a moan leaves her mouth. My pet is beautiful like this, completely falling apart in front of me. Removing my fingers from her pussy, I move my mouth to take their place and begin lapping her to get all that I can in my mouth. Feeling her cum dripping onto my chin is the best feeling. Her salty release coats my tongue. I need more.

Making sure I get every last drop out of her, I pinch her clit with my now free hand, "Ah, Jaxson," my name falling off her lips is intoxicating.

She bucks against me one last time as her orgasm begins to die down. I can hear her heavy breathing.

Lily lets go of my hair and rests her arms next to her body. I finish cleaning her up with my mouth and put her panties back in place. Bring my lips to them. I kiss her now covered pussy, breathing in her delicious scent once more before pulling back.

Moving back to my spot, I bring myself back out from under the blankets.

My pet's eyes are closed, her chest still heaving from the orgasm I just gave her.

Placing my hand on her cheek, I move her head to face me. My pet tries to open her eyes, but just barely, "Shh, you sleep in today, pet, you need the rest. You've earned it." I instruct her.

Bringing my lips to hers, I kiss her, savoring her soft lips against mine, while leaving some of her cum behind. As I pull back, she licks her lips and smiles back at me as her eyes begin to close again. "Thank you, Jaxson."

Leaning over, I kiss her one last time on her forehead before rolling out of bed and leaving her behind to rest.

CHAPTER 16

LILY

It was late morning by the time I finally woke up and got ready for the day. Jaxson actually let me sleep in for once, after giving me the best present this morning. I love orgasms. And that man's tongue? His skill is top tier. I always thought getting oral would be odd and uncomfortable, but it's everything but that. Then he let me sleep in. Though I will never tell him how much I appreciated it, the man doesn't need a bigger ego. But I really fucking needed it, especially after last night's attack. They always drain all my energy. Shit, I still can't believe I had one over my cousin being late. What the fuck is wrong with me? I mean, I know exactly what's wrong: I'm getting attached. Jaxson will just end up leaving once he thinks I'm fine and can fend for myself, just like my parents. And I know I will just break all over again. I can't lose another person. I won't make it. I'm barely making it now.

Shaking my head of the thoughts, I look at the time. It's midafternoon. Still a few more hours until Jaxson gets home and I'm bored out of my fucking mind. Laying on the couch and mindlessly scrolling on my phone just isn't cutting it. Plus, the longer I lay here, the more my mind is polluted with the stories it is telling itself. They say silence is a killer. It is.

I know some stories aren't true, but I always listen to the noise.

Fuck this, maybe I'll try going for a walk again. Everyone always preaches *'being out in nature helps clear the mind'* or *'it's so peaceful'* and since I don't have my pills anymore, I am running low on options on how to find some fucking peace.

Getting up from the couch and walking to the door, I yell, "Jinx, I'll be back soon!" Then head out.

There's a park down the road from the trailer. I'll just go there.

Ok, I am doing this. I am walking to calm myself. To be one with nature. To pass the time, because I'm really fucking bored.

Making my way down the gravel road, rocks crunch beneath my converse clad feet. It's a beautiful day. I am in black jean shorts and a tank top, and the sun feels fantastic against my skin. I can hear birds off in the distance chirping, but it's still too quiet.

My mind starts going at it again, and I know I'm definitely getting attached to Jax. Even though it's only been a few days, I look forward to when he gets home. I love pissing him off and I am only just learning all his buttons to press. The man is so easy to work up. He pierced my nipple with a nail, so it's the least I can do in return. And even though his approach isn't conventional; buying me weed to get off the pills or waking me up every morning before he goes to work so I can crawl to him like his good pet and suck his cock. At least he's here and consistent.

I stop for a moment, take a deep breath in and let the fresh air hit my lungs. It does feel nice, but I don't know if this walk thing is really working. My brain still has me analyzing everything.

I'm almost at the park, and I can see it has swings, a bench, and a kid's jungle gym. The park is old and you can tell it's not well maintained. As I get closer, I notice there's rust on the metal swing chains and it's starting on the slide. My parents never brought me here. Or if they did, I don't remember. Which is probably a good thing. I'm in no mental state to be taking a walk down memory lane right now.

Making my way through the overgrown grass, I head over to the wooden benches and take a seat.

There's no one else around. What do people do when they sit? I've taken in the fresh air. I'm outside being one with nature. I think I am enjoying it. Maybe? I can hear the birds better here and their songs are beautiful. But what else do I do here? I always see older people outside sitting. What do they know that I don't? What am I supposed to do next?

Shit. I know!

Pulling out my phone, I click on the camera app and flip it to selfie mode. Holding it away from me, I plant on the fakest smile I can muster up, like I'm having the best fucking time ever. As though sitting on the old wooden park bench, which is giving my ass splinters, is the highlight of my life. And I add one of my new best friends to make sure this high level of happiness gets across in this photo—my middle finger. My phone is angled perfectly, so I start snapping. Moving my head to give different angles is a must. I may have been sheltered growing up, but I know we always need photo options to pick from.

After taking a few more, it's time to go through them. Scrolling, they are all pretty good. But this one here really screams everything I am looking for, all in one shot.

My eyes are squinting, a big closed-mouth smile, nose scrunched up, and my cheekbones high. My finger did its part–she looks fabulous. This is the one.

Going to my texts, I find my sweet, dear cousin's text chain, open our chat, attach the photo, and add the caption *'I hate you :)'* before pressing send.

Fuck, this feels good. This is why people walk. I get it now!

A few minutes pass when my phone vibrates, and Jaxson's name is on my screen. I can't wait.

Sliding it open, his reply has me bursting with laughter,

'Good, but you will pay for this later, pet' plus a middle finger emoji.

Shit, I haven't laughed in what feels like forever. And there was nothing particularly hilarious about the reply. It was typical Jaxson. But maybe that's why it's funny?

I'm so screwed. Placing my phone back in my short's pocket, I bury my face in my hands.

Please, he can't leave me.

CHAPTER 17

JAX

It's been over a week since I gave Lily her new piercing and found her in a full on anxiety attack in the living room. I have started to put some structure back into her life. She needs it. She needs to feel like she has a purpose, so she doesn't drown into herself again with worry and fear. I wake her up before I leave work every day. My pet takes care of me, or I take care of her. Her pussy is often my treat before breakfast, sucking her clit so hard that it makes her back arch. It's one of my favorite things. How her body reacts to me. I know she finds comfort in what we have between us.

We both do. We feel like we belong to each other, even though we don't say it aloud.

She reminds me about how much she hates me before I head off to work and I always say good. At least she is feeling something instead of nothing and I will take this version of her over the other any day. I bought cleaning supplies the other night, and each day I ask her to try to do one room or area in the trailer. All this is to keep her busy, not because I am too lazy to do shit myself. Otherwise, she would just sit and watch tv all day. That isn't healthy, either. I encourage her to go for walks and get some fresh air. Sometimes she will send me pictures while she's out in the nearby park. The odd one will be a selfie, usually including her middle finger. It always makes me laugh. Even though I don't think that's the reaction she was aiming for, I still find them funny each time I get one.

Lily has also found some recipes online; the last few nights, she has surprised me with dinner. I was shocked that it was actually half decent. Not knowing if she could cook, I didn't know what to expect. I'm just so fucking happy that my cousin is starting to look healthy again.

I sleep in her room each night, on that tiny double bed with the fucking cat. Sometimes, I play with my pet at night. I like to see how far I can take it and test how much restraint she has. Some nights she moves or moans too much, and I stop. Leaving her wet and needy while I go to sleep. She isn't allowed to touch herself afterwards when that happens. I haven't caught her breaking those rules yet. But if she did, I would gladly punish her for it.

Sometimes we just crash and don't play. I work outside all day, in the hot heat. It can be exhausting; all I can do is shower, eat and close my eyes to sleep beside her. I haven't been home late since that day either. I can't do that to her ever again. As much as I like having fun with her, her mental health is my priority. I never want to see her like that because of me. It nearly broke me that night. All over my stupidity. I should have known that her mind would convince her that I had left rather than being late. That I had left her like her parents.

It's Sunday. I always have Sundays off. I need one day to recharge for my own sanity.

We are both sitting on her front steps. She is on the step below me and we are smoking a joint and I am drinking a beer. The day is beautiful, and we are just enjoying ourselves. I have noticed a difference in her since I switched her weed out. The stuff those fuck-heads had her smoking before was heavy on the THC and low on the CBD. It's the exact opposite of what she needed for her anxiety. The guy I know specializes in medicinal marijuana. Selling it to local medical dispensaries to help people with mental health and other conditions, such as cancer and seizures. To me, it's not a drug. It's a medicine that legitimately helps people.

Lily's attacks aren't happening daily anymore, life is starting to come back into her, from the look in her eyes to the color of her skin. It's not as pasty and deathly looking as it was before. She isn't cured, she never will be. Her mental health will always be a part of her. But if this can help reduce the amount of anxiety she experiences, or make the attacks she has less severe and frequent, I will forever be grateful. She hasn't complained about not having the pills since that night, either. I wasn't sure how hooked those fuckers got her, and I was worried about withdrawal symptoms. But she must have been fairly new to taking them. I haven't asked about school or her parents; she is still fragile and I won't push for more details right now. Another thing I have been worried about is her need to be numb and feel nothing, but she hasn't made any comments about that either. That speaks volumes, and I will take it.

Speaking of those idiots, they have also stayed away. It's for the best they've listened. I would have no issue making them disappear if they ever tried to contact her again. Working in construction, I have plenty of options on where to bury a body. Even if I didn't, I know people. The thought of ruining them brings a smile to my face. But my plotting is interrupted by Lily's neighbor, Janice. "Afternoon you two. Lily, any word from your parents yet?"

Go fuck yourself Janice. None of this is any of your business. I take a hit of my joint and blow it out at her. Dumb bitch. Then chase it with my beer.

I feel the anxiety at the mention of her parents radiating off Lily. She moves closer to my leg, with my foot on the same step she is sitting on. She reaches around my short clad legs and holds onto me. I start to rub the top of her head; all of this helps to calm her. I love that I can comfort her like this when she needs it. I will always protect her and be there for her. And I will fuck anyone up who dares try to hurt her again.

Before I can tell Janice to get fucked, Lily beats me to it. It's for the best, she's more polite these days than I am.

"No. No update, sorry, Janice." She mumbles. I hate that she just apologized to this nosey cunt. It should be the other way around.

Janice just nods and goes to her car.

"Lil, you don't need to apologize to that bitch. You didn't do anything to her, and you don't owe her shit." I whisper. I'm pissed off, but I don't want to rattle her more.

As each day goes by, even though it's been just a

short time, bits and pieces of the old Lily are coming back out. But I know it will never be like it was. She has been through hell and back. Seeing these glimpses of her starting to show again gives me comfort that she may come out of this not completely fucked up.

"I know, Jaxson, but if I didn't say what I did, she would just keep asking questions. I just wanted her to leave," her voice trembles. The need to push this a bit more is strong. We've danced around this topic, but since Janice already stirred the pot, I may as well take the opportunity myself.

"Pet, can you tell me what happened? With your parents."

Lily nudges in closer to me, and there's no room left between up. She's so close, I can feel her heart racing. She shakes her head and closes her eyes, her pain written on her face.

"Shh, pet. I'm here. I will always be here. But I need you to tell me. If I am going to help you, I need to know. Please, Lil." I plead while also trying to soothe her at the same time.

She opens her eyes and looks up at me. They are filled with grief and sadness.

"Jax, can you do something for me?"

"Anything," I mean it.

"Make me forget, I need to forget."

I know exactly what she means, and if this will

help, I will do it. We haven't gone this far before, but I would do anything for this girl.

"We can't run from this forever. But I will do anything in my power to help you." I sigh.

She nods; she knows she will have to tell me everything... eventually. I will keep bringing it up until she does, but I will never force it. I just want her to start to become comfortable with the idea of saying it all out loud. To know I won't leave too. She will never be alone again.

Putting my joint out, I stand up and put my hand out for her to grab. She follows my lead and takes it without hesitation.

"Come on, cousin." I encourage as I turn around and lead us toward the bedroom, through the front door and down the hall. I pass her room and continue going straight down the hall.

"Whoa, where are we going?"

Turning around, I look at her while still holding her one hand. "Fuck them. They don't deserve your respect. They don't serve your hope or happiness. Fuck them, Lil." I say with a smirk.

"Now, follow me, and let me take care of you. Make you forget, if only for a little while."

"Ok. Yeah." She still sounds nervous. But I got her. I won't let her fall anymore.

We take the last few steps before we are outside of

her parents' bedroom door. Without hesitation, I turn the handle, open the door, and lead us inside.

This isn't going to be sweet. This is going to be hard and rough. I begin to remove my clothes. Peeling off my shirt as my pet watches. Next, I take off my shoes, remove my socks, then finally take my shorts and underwear off. Leaving them in a pile at my feet.

"Do you like what you see, pet?" I chuckle, completely naked, catching her checking me out. She is always admiring my ink, and I know she likes to draw, so I understand her appreciation for art, but I haven't seen her sketch since I have been here.

She just shakes her head and smiles at me. Then follows suit removing her converse, tank top, jean shorts, and panties. She isn't wearing a bra, and her breasts are smaller but perky. Her piercing is still in place, she is so beautiful. And I am so fucking proud of her.

We both take a step toward each other to close the gap between us and immediately, our lips connect. I deepen the kiss, bringing my tongue to her lips and she parts them easily for me. At the same time, placing my hands on her hips and start backing her up until she hits the edge of the bed. Grabbing underneath her arms, I disconnect our kiss and throw her onto the bed. Her eyes land on my already hard cock. I can't wait to get inside of her, but first I walk to where my shorts are and grab the condom I have stashed inside of my wallet. There will be no foreplay. I can't wait another minute to get inside her pussy. I tear open the foil, throw the wrapper on the ground and roll the rubber up my shaft. Looking back at her, I see the disappointment on her face. "Condoms until you're on birth control, pet." I am firm on this. Neither of us needs a kid in this world yet. And she knows I'm right.

I kneel on the bed, and she spreads her legs for me to get in between. Wasting no time, I line my cock up to her entrance and slam myself into her tight pussy. Her back arches, and a loud moan escapes her mouth. I don't start moving yet, giving her a moment to adjust to my large size. Watching her until I see her relax, and knowing it's ok to start. I grip the bed's headboard with one hand and bring one of her legs over my shoulder with the other. "This won't be gentle, pet. I won't take it easy on you. I will leave my mark inside of you. I will fuck you until you can't take it anymore, and even then, I may not stop."

"I will never want you to stop, cousin. Fuck them all." She says with a smirk. This girl is going to kill me.

With that, I start to pound into her. Showing no restraint or control, just unfiltered, raw obsession. I own her. My pet. My whore. Mine.

"No one will fuck this hole other than me. ONLY. FUCKING. ME." I snarl.

"Only you," she moans back.

I continue slamming my cock into her, "Good girl, you are taking me so well." The headboard is banging against the wall, nothing but background noise. My focus is on her. How her body responds to me. How with each thrust a moan escapes her. How she needs her hands on me; both are on my chest rubbing my skin. She never breaks contact.

She opens her eyes and pants. "I can feel your piercing rubbing inside of me; it feels amazing, Jaxson. Don't stop."

Smiling back at her, "Then it's doing what it's supposed to. I will never stop, pet. You are being such a good little whore for your cousin."

I start moving quicker when I feel her walls start to grip me; her orgasm is building. Her leg shakes in my hold, and her back starts arching off the bed. I can't take my eyes off her tiny perky breasts, wearing my mark on her nipple. Her pussy begins to milk my cock, and I keep moving, panting now as I chase my own release.

"Ah, Jaxson." She whimpers.

"Jaxson, I want to be your favorite. Let me be your favorite."

"Always, pet. No one else but you. My perfect whore, my favorite toy." Her cum begins to coat my cock and I follow. Unable to hold back anymore, I let my orgasm join hers. The tingle moves down my spine and I start shooting cum into the condom as she continues to milk me within the vise her pussy has created. I let a grunt of my own out while still pounding into her, so we both get the most out of this. Sweat is dripping down my forehead as I start to slow down, but always keeping my eyes on her, watching her body, her pussy, my cock moving in and out of it. Lily is also experiencing the same effects. Together, we are glistening.

Slowing my movements, I let go of the headboard. I'm shocked I didn't tear it off. Releasing my grip on my pet's leg and sliding my cock out of her, I roll to lay beside her. I can feel the heat radiating off her body. This sex was fast and hard, but there were also a thousand unspoken words said during it. Our dark and depraved souls have collided. I felt it the moment I slid my cock inside of her pussy and then again with each thrust.

"Lil, can you do something for me?" I wonder if she will go for it.

"Yeah, of course."

"Go into my pants pocket and grab my switchblade. I want you to mark me. Like I marked you." She looks at me, unsure if I'm serious, waiting for a moment to see if I'll change my mind. I won't.

She gets up quickly, looks in one pocket, and then the other until she finds it. She brings it back and hands it to me. As I lay still, I open the metal blade and place it back in her hand.

"Do it, pet. Anywhere you want. I want your mark on me, too." I encourage her.

She pokes the tip with her finger, drawing a droplet of blood, and places it in my mouth to suck. I do. It's just as intoxicating as the first time I tasted it, if not even more so.

She places her hand on my chest, rubbing it gently from my collarbone to my abdomen.

Her hand lands on my pelvis, "Here. I want it here."

"Do it."

Using the blade's sharp tip, Lily slowly starts cutting my skin. I want to watch, but I also want it to be a surprise once she's done. So, I close my eyes and just feel as she continues. It doesn't hurt. I fucking love this. With each movement, I try to decipher what she could be doing, but I have no idea. It's not long before my thoughts are interrupted, though.

"Ok. I'm done," she whispers and drops the bloody blade to the bed.

I open my eyes and look down to see *'pet'* carved into my pelvis.

"It's perfect," I praise her as I continue to look at it. Some blood is dripping out of each letter. But I let it run down my body.

I reach my arm out and grab the back of her head, bringing her lips to mine, and kiss her like it's my last day. Sucking the oxygen from her lungs to mine. She fucking owns me.

Breaking the kiss, Lily whispers against my lips, "Stay here."

"Ok, pet," whispering back to her.

She gets up, still naked, and leaves the room. I hear her rummaging around in her room, then it goes silent. What is she doing?

Lil walks back into the room, puts her long dark hair up in a ponytail, and she has a white envelope in her hand.

She kneels back onto the bed and crawls over to me, looking terrified. My guard goes up instantly. What the fuck is going on?

"Pet, what is it? What's wrong?" I ask as I sit up and hold her face.

She places a comforting hand on one of mine. "I want you to read this."

Then puts the envelope down in front of me on her parents' bed.

"Ok, I'll read it. Will you stay with me while I do?"

Her eyes are no longer looking at me. She has them closed and nods. I let her get away without using her words this time. Whatever this is, it has her shaken. Her hand trembles against mine. She lets go of my hand and clasps both hers together on her lap.

I remove my hands from her face, grab the envelope which says 'Lily' on the front and open it. I find a piece of folder paper inside. Taking it out and placing the empty envelope back down, I unfold the paper to see a note written on it,

Lily,

You have probably noticed by now we aren't home.

We left, Lil. We won't be back.

Raising you for the last 17 years has given us the greatest joy. We are so proud of you. We know you will do great things. Use your art to take you there.

It's our time to live now. Our job here is done.

The lot fees on the trailer are paid for the next two months. It should get you to the summer and your birthday.

From there, you'll need to get a job once school is over and keep paying them on your own.

I have canceled our phones. You won't be able to reach us. Please don't bother to try. We didn't take this decision lightly. This was necessary for us.

We need to do this for ourselves. To find ourselves as individuals again and not just parents.

We know you're probably panicking right now, Lil.

Just breathe, my girl. You are strong!

We love you always,
Mom & Dad.

These pieces of shit. I want to murder them. I want to torture them slowly so they feel every ounce of pain I inflict. And I will remind them that the pain they are feeling is nothing compared to the pain they caused their little girl. The pain they have caused her can never be forgiven. I will never be forgotten. If I see them, that is precisely what I will do—bleed them dry. Cut them into little pieces and feed them to the pigs. So no trace of their disgusting existence in this world remains. I don't give a shit if they are my aunt and uncle.

They are dead to me.

To us!

Chapter 18

Lily

The sex was incredible. I have never had sex sober before, and it felt more intimate. But there was something more than that with Jaxson. I felt like a goddess. I felt like he actually wanted me, and the connection we have is undeniable at this point. His piercing rubbing inside of me with each thrust made me cum harder and faster than ever before with Luke. I feel safe with Jax. I just need him to want to keep me. He has to keep me. He let me mark myself on his beautifully decorated skin. I can't be left again. I don't think I will survive it this time. At first, I was pissed off that he would insert himself into something he knew nothing about. But I was barely surviving. He saw that before I was able to. Jax has given me purpose again. He cares about my health, and he helps me with my anxiety. This may not be normal, but it works for us.That's why I decided to let him see the letter. After everything, there was no way I could not show him it.

The familiar feeling of my heart beating rapidly against my chest, the fear of rejection lingering. I pass him the letter to read.

I keep my eyes closed while he does. I can't bear to see if he is disgusted by me after this. If my parents didn't want to stay with me, why would he? If I am thinking these thoughts, how could he not be? I can't take sitting here in silence anymore. I quickly open my eyes, shifting myself off the bed and run into the bathroom, not bothering to close the door behind me.

My breathing has picked up. It's uneven. My vision narrows, and flickers of light flash in my eyes. I'm starting to spiral. I have been doing so well these past few days, but that letter. Even just holding it killed me inside. But he needed to see it. I don't want to hide this from him anymore. But I am fucking terrified at the same time. I plug the bath drain and turn on the taps, needing to escape. Needing silence. I don't wait for the bath to fill; going in and sitting immediately, letting the water rise around me. My brain starts with its narrative; *He didn't chase you. He didn't follow you. He doesn't want you.*

I don't want to listen to it, but it could be right. He fucked me. I was his whore, his pet. He no longer has a use for me. I will never be worthy of love or a family. My biggest fear is coming to life.

The water has reached my waist, and I can't wait any longer. I lower myself underneath it and scream. My eyes are closed, but I feel the air bubbles leaving my mouth as I let it all out. Once I am out of oxygen, I close my mouth and don't get up. My lungs start to contract, and I can feel my chest muscles tighten with each one. Before I can get to the point where I black out, I suddenly feel hands under my armpits, lifting me up out of the water. My eyes open and I gasp for air. My entire body is out of the water now and I feel the chill of the air against my skin almost instantly. It makes me shiver. A hand goes to my head and I feel a hard chest against my face. I take in my surroundings and see I'm on the bathroom floor. Jaxson has me nuzzled against his bare chest. He is holding me so tightly in his strong arms, we couldn't get any closer if we tried. His head is resting on mine, he is rocking us back and forth and whispering to me, "It's ok. I got you, Lil. It's ok." Over and over again.

I don't move, just needing to stay in his arms like this and listen to his words of reassurance. I want to believe them, but I don't know if I can.

We stay like this for a while, maybe he does care, feeling safe I almost falling asleep in his arms. It's a mixture of the sex, and the anxiety attack, that has caused my exhaustion.

"Lily. You are not staying in this place anymore."

"Where am I supposed to go?"

Is he kicking me out? Does he not want me anymore? Why did I have to get attached? I knew this would happen. Fuck!

"Hey, stop whatever it is you're thinking. I can feel your mind racing a million miles an hour. You're done here. We are going to pack your shit, and you and that cat are going to come home with me."

My eyes snap open as I continue to lean into his bare chest.

"But what if my parents come back and I'm not here? I need to be here." I plead with him. I'm not thinking rationally.

"Lil, they don't deserve you. Let them come back and find you gone. If I have it my way, they will never see you again. Those selfish bastards are not worthy of being known as your parents anymore. They are nothing. They're no one. I will fucking slaughter them if I ever see them again, for what they have done to you." His words are filled with rage.

"And what, you think you deserve me? You want me all to yourself, is that it? Because you feel sorry for me? I don't need anyone feeling sorry for me." It's the truth. I don't need or want anyone to do things because they feel sorry for me. I just want to be wanted, to be needed, to be loved.

"Lil, I think you are the strongest person I know. You took care of yourself the only way you could. Now let me take care of you, please. I don't deserve you. I never will, but that doesn't stop me from needing you. I need you Lily. I own you. You are mine, but you also own me," he confesses.

I don't know what to say. I feel overwhelmed, but in a good way. My eyes water and I look up at him and react the only way I know how. "I hate you," I say with a smile.

He throws his head back and laughs, "I hate you too, pet. Now, let's get off this fucking bathroom floor, get dressed, and start packing up your stuff. We aren't staying here another night. Fuck them, fuck this place. We are going home."

As much as I want to fight him on this, I don't. I know I can't see the logic in it right now, not when I am like this. A few hours from now I will. I know that once I've calmed down, I will understand what he is saying is true. He's never given me a reason to doubt him. Since getting here, Jaxson has only ever wanted to take care of me and protect me. I trust him with everything. Even my heart.

"Ok, Jaxson." Tilting my head up, I seal it with a

kiss just under his chin, then snuggle back into him. He is my safe place.

JAX

I fucking love this girl.

It's all I think as we sit here like this, naked and still on the floor. She has agreed to come home with me. Our home now. And when we get home, we are burning this fucking letter in our firepit. Her parents are lucky it's just the letter I'm going to burn. We should burn this whole fucking trailer to the ground.

I feel tears well in my eyes. I don't fight it. Between reading the letter, finding her trying to escape, and now agreeing to come home, I've turned into a fucking pussy.

Blinking, I let one droplet slide down my cheek into Lily's hair. She is snuggled up against my bare chest, still wet from the bath. I never want her to feel this way again. Like she needs to escape reality. Or like she isn't wanted. I will always take care of my pet. Always support her on this journey. I will always want her. She's mine and I'll fucking destroy anyone who stands in her way. I will not allow this to define her.

She owns me. If there was ever any doubt of that, it's gone now.

"Our bed at home is much bigger than the tiny one

we have been sharing in your room." Lily doesn't respond, she just listens.

"Our place isn't big, but it's home. We have a back-yard with a fire pit and patio. I don't know if you're into gardening or whatever, but you can do what you want with the yard. I will stock up the kitchen with whatever you need. I know you like testing those recipes you find online. We can get you supplies for your drawings. I saw some in your room. You have fucking talent, Lily. Shit, redecorate the place for all I care. Make it our home. Don't be afraid of touching shit either, it's ours now. As long as you're always there when I get home, I don't fucking care what you do. Would it be a plus if I walked in and you were naked, dripping wet and desperate to fuck me? Shit, on your knees for me, like my good pet. Abso-fucking-lutely."

She giggles and I smile into her hair, taking in her scent of vanilla and coconut.

"I'll always be your good pet. Your favorite whore. Let's go home, Jaxson."

LILY

The hot summer sun is shining on my face. I have spread out a thin blanket on the grass outside in our backyard, and I am laid out on it, wearing a black string bikini top and cut-off jean shorts. My hair is in a pony, I debated cutting it after everything last year. Start fresh and all. But I like how Jaxson pulls it during sex, so I decided against cutting it. The thought brings me back to last night, his muscular tattooed body fucking me from behind and his strong hand pulling my hair with the other wrapped around my throat. It wasn't a shock to either of us. I like breath play during sex.

I rub my neck at the thought of it and smile.

Last spring, after I moved in with Jaxson and once I felt like I could handle it, I returned to school to get my high school diploma, taking online classes to finish what I'd missed. I was so excited and relieved when I took my exams and passed, knowing how far I have come this past year.

I spiraled after my parents left. Hard. My brain was telling me lies that I was believing. But when you're deep in it, dealing with all of that plus your mental health, all of that is bound to happen. You believe what your mind is telling you. There is no reasoning with us during attacks or episodes; we do not see rationally until afterward and can reflect on it. bought a few self-help books to help better understand it all, and did loads of research online about reputable mental health professional sites. I know I will never be at a hundred percent, and I don't need to be. Because I'm finally happy like this. I have a great fucking life now.

But I do want to understand my mental health better and be proactive instead of reactive about it moving forward.

I learned a few additional techniques on how to handle myself when I feel one coming on, aside from finding comfort from Jaxson when I am able to snuggle into his leg and he rubs my head. They also don't happen as often now. Jax has been such a help with that, ensuring I have a routine in my life. I keep busy with things I like to do. But if I do feel one coming on I let him know, and I start my breathing exercises, turn on my calming sounds app and let it ride. I know the lies aren't true, and I remind myself of that when my brain tells me them. It doesn't always work, but it helps.

Sometimes if Jax is home during one, he will even lay with me as I go through the motions. Jinx always sits at my feet, and the weed still helps, too. All of this together has made such a difference in my life. I will forever be grateful for this man and his support in me.

We haven't been back to the trailer park since that weekend. We packed everything up that I needed and never looked back. Jinx likes it here, too. More space and a yard to play in with birds to chase. I don't miss the park either. But that is all in the past now, along with my parents.

Sometimes I will get calls from an 'unknown number.' But I never answer it. If it is them, I don't want to know or speak to them. The first couple of times, I was tempted to answer. I was curious about what they could possibly say to me after all this time. What excuses, and what reasons they had. It used to cause my mind to run rampant. Now, I don't care. They don't deserve me. They left me; I didn't leave them, and now they will pay for their actions. There are always consequences. They no longer get to have part of me. That is their loss because I am a fucking amazing person. They are the ones missing out, not me. I actually feel sorry for them. They threw our life away to be selfish. I know parents deserve to have their own identity outside of being mom and dad, but not how they did it. Now they are alone, with only each other and no more family.

A week or so after we left the park, we shared what happened with my uncle, Jaxson's dad, and my dad's brother. He's also vowed to never allow them back in his life. Bad behavior doesn't get rewarded, he said. We also told him that we were a couple. He was so excited and happy–if we are happy; he is happy–that's what he told us. I call him dad now. He has never judged or questioned us; only showing us his love and affection.

I have also started drawing again. Jax even set up the spare room with an old desk and lamp for me, so I have my own space when I feel the need to be creative. I missed it so much and didn't realize how much until I started again. I also started a blog; posting some of what I draw and speak openly about my mental health. I go under a fake name; I am not that brave. The thought of using my own stresses me out. But I want others to know that they are not alone. I also clarify that what works for me and my particular situation is a part of my approach in managing it. Each person is on their own journey and should do what works for them and for others to remember that when offering support or tips to others. I also encourage them to never be afraid of contacting professionals for help, additional resources and assistance. There are so many of us also dealing with this daily, and there is no shame in asking for help. I have been overwhelmed by all the positive comments and responses I've gotten. At first I kept the blog to myself; I wasn't sure if I would ever share with Jaxson my little side project. I felt very protective over it, and what ifs' started to enter my mind when I did think of telling him. What if he didn't approve? What if he didn't like it? Then I remembered he may not like other people very much, but he has never given me a reason to doubt his support for me. So one day, I opened it on my phone and threw it in his lap while he was watching TV on the couch. After I ran away to our room. The waiting killed me. It felt like ages until he came in.

"Pet, why did you throw this at me and run away?" He asked, while holding up my phone.

I knew I was in for it.

I explained it all to him and he threw the phone back on the bed. I wasn't sure what that meant, but then he walked over to me, picked me up, and held me against his chest as he took my spot on the bed. He just kept whispering how proud he was of me. How far I had come and never to be afraid of sharing things like this with him. The reassurance meant everything. Then he edged me for three days as punishment for hiding this from him. He was right, too. There was no need for me to worry or be afraid.

I'm lost in my thoughts of all these beautiful memories when I hear a deep voice shout, "Lil, you back here?" He's home! And early.

I get up from my blanket and run toward the driveway, where I find him lighting up a joint.

That took no time at all.

"Tough day?"

He laughs at me. "Yeah, you could say that. A couple of guys called in sick, so I had to do their shit, and now I'm behind on some of the bullshit paperwork I have to do. I swear to fuck, I'm going to bash their heads in the next time I see them. I know they aren't sick. They went out last night."

Jax is still a caveman. You should see it if we are out and someone looks at me with 'they want to fuck you eyes' as he calls it. I'll never condone it out loud, but I like it when he gets defensive and protective of me.

The construction company Jax works for promoted him to site foreman. He works so hard, and I wasn't shocked when he came home a few months ago with the news. He deserves it. Jaxson gets to run his own project sites now. They aren't big, but he's the boss, which is a massive accomplishment.

"Poor bossman," I mock as I walk into his embrace.

"Yeah, poor bossman. Can you come in with me tomorrow and help with some of it?"

I like when I get to go to work with him. Sometimes when a job is just starting, there are a lot of invoices, permits and clerical work, so I help him part-time with the administrative stuff. I really like it.

He has even mentioned a few times starting his own residential construction company, and I could be his office manager, since having learnt so much helping him on sites. But we will see. There isn't a big rush for it or for me to figure out what I want from life; I only just turned nineteen. We still have so much time to figure everything out. For now, we are happy, and if new opportunities happen, we will go from there. Never say never.

"I suppose so." Acting like it's such a hassle for me. I can still be a tad bratty.

"You suppose so, hmm?" He reaches for my breast and grabs my nipple, causing me to flinch. I still have the nail in it from when he pierced it. He loves doing this to mess with me. But I like the pain. He knows it.

"Pet, do you want to rethink that answer?"

"I mean, I don't have plans tomorrow, so I guess I could?" I tease back, knowing exactly what I'm doing.

"Be a good little whore and help bossman out. You can even wear what you got on now. I'll keep the guys out of the trailer. This is only for me," he says before taking another hit.

What is he up to? I don't think we are talking about his work anymore. I look at him with curiosity. He leans down and kisses me. I part my lips for him, and he blows the smoke in my mouth and I inhale it into my lungs. I feel his hard cock pressing against me through his pants. I pull back slightly and exhale, blowing the remaining smoke into the air around us.

I whisper against his lips while looking into his beautiful mismatched eyes, "I hate you."

He whispers back, with a smirk, "I hate you too."

JAX

Yes, to everything she just said. I'm so fucking proud of my pet. She's the strongest person I know. After that final night at the trailer, we came home and burnt that fucking letter her parents left. I asked Lily if she wanted to do it alone, but she insisted I stayed. She wanted to end that chapter of her life and start the new one with me by her side. I held her tight as we watched it burn into ashes. Those words haunting her mind were gone. Nothing more than a memory now.

The next morning she woke up different. Lighter. The dark cloud moving away from overtop of her. She's been through hell and back. I've been here by her side cheering her on, but Lily's done all the hard work herself.

And yeah, I am still a 'caveman' as she calls me. But she's mine until my last breath. And I'll be damned if another fucker thinks they can look at her like she's fresh meat.

But looking at her now, standing in front of me, my pet is looking fucking delicious. Wearing her tiny black bathing suit top, barefoot and in those cut off jean shorts with her ass cheeks peeking out of the bottom. I need to play. My dick is already hard as I hold her close.

"Pet, go stand at the hood of the truck. Hands on the hood." She looks up at me and smiles. Then takes the joint out of my hand and takes a hit of her own before putting it out and walking to the truck's hood. Following her, I start unbuttoning my pants. Lil is bent over just how I like her. I stand behind her and pull her shorts down. Then, slipping my finger inside her panties, I find my pet is already soaked. Taking my hard cock out, I move her panties to the side, line myself up to her perfect pussy, which is dripping for me, and thrust into her.

If anyone were to see us, they would think I was just standing behind her through the truck windows. They would have no idea I was fucking her until she couldn't feel her legs anymore. Until it was just my hard cock holding her up. Grabbing her hips for better control, I whisper into her ear,

"Pet, if you're too loud, the neighbors may hear. I need you to stay quiet."

Lily nods her head.

"Words pet. I need to hear your words."

"I understand," she responds softly.

"Such a good little whore you are for me, aren't you?"

I continue to fuck her tight pussy like it's our first time. A frenzy always overcomes us. We will never get enough. Lily started birth control shortly after coming home so we can fuck bare with minimal worry now. I had never done that before her and it's the most incredible feeling being able to feel her cum dripping down my cock, knowing I'm the one who made this happen is so fucking addictive. Feeling my cock ring move against her g-spot as I move in and out of her. This is home.

I feel her walls start to tighten around me, and I bring my thumb to her asshole and tease it. Circling it slowly before sticking it in her. Lily loves the full feeling this gives her just before climaxing. With that she lets a tiny moan out, I let it slide since she's been doing so good.

"Such a good whore. My fucking whore. Taking

my cock so well. You like when I play with your tight hole, don't you, pet? My perfect whore."

That final bit of praise triggers her. As I feel her body tremble and her orgasm hits, I pull my thumb out which only further intensifies it. Lily's back arches, and her cum starts to drench my cock. Her walls begin to milk me, clamping around my cock like a vise. I continue to thrust into her as hard and fast as I can. We don't do slow. We are hard and rough. No mercy and we love seeing how far we can push the limits. As I feel my own orgasm hit. My cum shoots out, coating her pussy, my release joins hers. I want all of it dripping out of her by the time we are done. She is mine.

I mark her with my cum as my piercing continues to rub inside her pussy. Pushing to maximize her orgasm, milking every last drop out of us until all Lily can see in her version are stars.

Reaching my hand out, I wrap my fingers around her delicate neck and thrust into her one more time as both of our orgasms fade. She's fucking beautiful like this. My needy whore.

"You did so good, pet. So fucking good."

"I liked this, cousin. Being exposed out here, not knowing if someone can see us or get caught."

"Would you like to do this again, pet?" My girl likes a little exhibition, apparently.

"Yes, please." Lily responds eagerly while catching

her breath. I let go of her throat and slowly pull out of her. Our cum instantly starts to drip out of her pussy. I use two fingers to push it back inside of her, then put her panties back in place.

Putting my cock back in my pants, I do them back up as she does the same with her shorts.

Lily turns around to face me, her eyes still dazed and hooded as she looks up at me, "I don't want you to clean up. I want you dripping us until the morning."

"Of course, Jaxson. I wouldn't dare." Saying as she smirks back up at me.

I fucking love this girl.

The End.

Acknowledgments

I hope you loved Lily & her caveman, Jaxson, as much as I loved writing them!

Lily's story hit close to home. I was able to describe her anxiety and depression by channeling my own. Mind you, mine are not as severe as hers. But when she was feeling an attack coming on, I felt it. When she would submerge herself underwater to escape, I would close my eyes and feel what she did in the silence.

These feelings, and all others described are not isolated to just Lily & I.

So so many people wake up and have to face their mental health daily. Some days are really fucking hard. Some days I just want to sleep all day. Some days are really exhausting, putting a smile on and facing the world. I call it '*the show*', if people can't see the illness they will never know it's there. Some days it would be easier to just give into the demons. But when we don't give in, we win. We are strong. We are fierce.

We are fucking Queens!

Always remember that! Always know it's ok to not be ok.

And NEVER be afraid to ask for help.

I did.

I am medicated and love it.

Without it, I wouldn't be ME! And I really love me.

Never be ashamed to love yourself.

You cannot please everyone all the time.

It's ok to scream from the rooftops about mental health.

To remove the stigma.

Fuck the stigma.

You are worthy. Your feelings are valid. You are never alone!

Thank you for tuning into my Ted Talk!

This book also wouldn't be here if...my gothic Queen K.L. Taylor-Lane didn't tell me... while I was drinking wine, instead of writing... to wine & write on my phone and see what happens.

I love her. So I listened and did it.

This is what happened! And I love it.

Mind you I had to drink each time I sat down to write this book after that. For creative purposes, of course! ;)

Thank you to all of YOU. For jumping onto this wild taboo filled ride with me. I am forever grateful for everything. Thank you for reading. Thank you for buying my books and DMing me with words of encouragement. THANK YOU!

To my Alpha and Betas - this is just the beginning. Thank you for all your help with getting my babies ready for the world!! You, taking time out of your day to help me, it doesn't go unnoticed and I value you all so much!

TikTok & ARC Team - I was overwhelmed by the response from everyone who wanted to join. I am just this baby dark romance taboo author. I did not expect this and y'all leave me speechless! Thank you. Thank you!!!!!

And to my editor Rae! You were able to capture the essence of Lily & Jaxson perfectly when going through the chaos I submitted to you! Thank you for being so good with me and them!!

I am so lucky to be surrounded by so many strong & independent females!

Until the next one babes!!
    -Kins

ABOUT THE AUTHOR

Kinsley is a Canadian, Dark Romance Author who dabbles in Taboo, Forbidden and is currently in her Horror Era. When she isn't plotting her next twisted book or watching true crime docs with her cats, you can find her working for the man. Reading. Or drinking wine while causing chaos with friends, let's not limit ourselves now. Make sure you follow Kins on her socials and sign up for her newsletter to see what is coming next!

authorkinsleykincaid.com

More From Kinsley

Forbidden

Let's Play - Freebie

Within the Shadows

Lessons from the Depraved

Haunted by the Devil

Taboo

Wrecked

Sutton Asylum

Dark Temptation: Part One

Ghost Dick; A Port Canyon Chronicle

Dark Temptation: Part Two

Sick Obsession - 2024

F*ck Me, Daddy; A Port Canyon Chronicle - TBD